# Keeping Secrets

by
Cat Shaffer

## Dedication

To my son, Mark Shaffer, and my good friend Susan Thompson, who challenged me to write this book. So good or bad, it's all your fault!

## Chapter One

Rik Hallowell hammered one metal fence post after another into the Colorado soil, the blows echoing through the still air. This one, he decided as he swung the sledge, was for his worthless brother living it up in Las Vegas while Rik slaved under the summer sun. The next was for his father, whose death had left Mom unprepared to handle four thousand acres of pasture and a thousand head of cattle. He pounded in another for his own conscience, the nagging voice that pushed him into temporarily swapping his life in San Francisco for this.

Rik moved in a steady rhythm along the sagging stretch of wire, setting post after post until he finished off the roll of barbed wire. Back at the ranch truck, he squinted at the sky. It was blue and cloudless, with no sign of that rain the television weatherman predicted. Naturally.

Sighing, he opened the top of the cooler in the truck bed and pulled out a bottle. Pulling off his battered black hat, he poured half a bottle of water over his head. The rest he drank down in long, thirsty gulps. Man, he was getting soft. Ten years ago, he would have made quick work of stringing fence that should have been fixed weeks ago. Yet he was both surprised and dismayed by how quickly the routine of the ranch had come back. Twenty-one years here made an indelible impression his new life couldn't wipe out.

He moved the truck down the line and returned to work with great reluctance. Now every savage twist he made as he moved from post to post represented something his family expected him to give up. His position as second in command at Domino Industries. The San Francisco condo he called home. His hard-fought place in an upper crust society of beautiful women and powerful men.

The sun was dropping by the time Rik stood back to study his handiwork, slapping the heavy leather gloves against his thigh in satisfaction. No more cattle would wander off now. He stretched, wincing at the ache in muscles unaccustomed to hard labor.

Tossing his equipment into the truck and climbing into the cab, he jolted down the dirt road dividing the Hallowell ranch from public grazing land. He drove slowly, searching for other weak places. One of the last things his father had done before keeling over of a heart attack was sign a federal lease on some of this grazing land. Now he had to deal with damned government red tape on top of his mother's constant worry over the place going belly-up.

Rik couldn't do much about Uncle Sam, but he managed to convince his mother to take a trip to her native Virginia to help her sister recover from hip surgery. With any luck, Aunt Lou's recuperation would last long enough for him to get this place back into shape, hire a manager and high-tail it back to civilization.

Preoccupied, driving into the afternoon sun, he didn't see the beige sedan parked sideways across the road until it was almost too late. He slammed on the brakes and stopped mere inches from the vehicle.

"What the hell do you think you're doing?" he shouted at the figure on the other side of the car.

No answer. A lost tourist picking a damned wildflower, he supposed. He slung open the door and climbed out, yelling as he walked toward the sedan.

"Miles of nothing and you stop in the middle of the road?"

He rounded the vehicle to see a woman cradling an Angus calf.

"I could have run over this little thing." Her voice was sharp, her face hidden by a broad-brimmed hat as she studied the small creature, legs splayed awkwardly to one side, its head in her lap. "I assume it's yours."

"It is. Thanks." Embarrassed by his misdirected anger, Rik bent down, cradled the small creature against his chest and carried it to his truck. He examined the calf with an assured touch, checking its breathing as he looked for injuries.

"Was it standing or down?" he called over his shoulder.

"Lying in the middle of the road. Which is why I parked like that. I didn't want either of us to get smooshed."

The calf snuffled against Rik's shirt. Although it was no doubt hungry and thirsty, it seemed fine. Rik could return it to the herd and let its mother take over.

"We've had some fence breaks, and it must have wandered through." He brushed his hands on the sides of his jeans and walked back to the woman. "The little fella got tuckered out and decided to rest, I suppose."

He meant to thank the stranger again, but the words froze in his throat when she pulled off her ball cap and sunglasses. Long strawberry blond hair tumbled to her shoulders. Hazel eyes stared at him from a tanned, oval face.

A thrill of recognition ran through him. It couldn't be her. Not here. Not after so many years.

"Randi?" He shoved the word through a suddenly dry throat. "Randi Coulsen?"

****

Heart pounding, Miranda watched shock and confusion play over Rikky's face. She recognized him the minute he left the truck. Seeing him again, so much the same and yet so different, shouldn't have been a surprise. After all, she knew his family ranch was near Armont. Yet here he was, so familiar, so…him. Could it really be ten years since she'd seen him? Ten years since he broke her heart and ruined her life?

As his stare weighed on her, she considered pretending she didn't remember him. Trouble was, she couldn't. She was lousy at emotional games. She had managed to forgive him, but there was no way to forget him.

"Hey, Rikky." She was pleased how neutral she sounded as the old nickname slid from her lips.

"It's Rik now. More grown-up for the business world." He grinned as if he was happy to see her.

She forced a small smile. "Oh, I understand. My mother pushed me to use Miranda. Says it sounds more dignified."

Thirty seconds of polite conversation so far. She was proud of herself, although she had no intention of sticking around. The last thing she wanted or needed was more exposure to Rik Hallowell.

When the calf bawled, she took advantage of the interruption.

"Someone's ready to go home," she said, smile in place. "See you around, Rik."

Nodding goodbye, she headed toward her government-issue car before the awkward, catching-up part of the conversation could begin. Rik fell in beside her, smelling strongly of sweat and calf and faintly of spicy, familiar cologne.

"So what brings you here?" he asked.

Miranda brushed a hand over her khaki uniform shirt. "Work. Counting anything that crosses my path. Wild horses, wild burros, bald eagles. Armadillos. I'm primarily part of a federal wildlife census team with a few other duties thrown in."

An eruption of song from Rik's worn jeans stopped the conversation. He fished in his pocket, yanked out his cell phone and glanced at the caller I.D.

"I have to take this," he apologized. "Business."

Miranda nodded. "Sure. See you around."

She climbed into the dusty vehicle, fired it up and watched through the rear view mirror as Rik dwindled to a tiny figure. In a county with more cows than people, why did it have to be his calf she found?

She sighed. Off and on, she wondered what it would be like to see him again. Of course, in those imaginings, she was in a glamorous dress, on the arm of someone rich, famous and gorgeous. She hadn't expected to come face to face with him sticky from hours in the sun, sweat and sun blocker replacing the aroma of the expensive perfume she fantasized him smelling as she coolly blew him off.

Too bad he hadn't gotten fat or wore glasses to hide those eyes, as blue as the sky that stretched above them. And how had she let the tenderness he showed toward the lost calf soften her heart? She had no business remembering how gentle his hands had been when they made love, how exquisite his touch could be...

"Knock it off, girl."

She spoke out loud, as if scolding herself could make her body quit remembering. She had at least an hour's worth of paperwork tonight, and she needed to email Brittani before bedtime.

Thank goodness her daughter loved staying with her grandparents. Miranda missed her terribly, but their future depended on this three-month assignment. If she did well, it could propel her into a supervisor's position. That meant a little higher salary, but more importantly, a regular nine-to-five schedule and time to get involved with PTA, Girl Scouts and everything else Brittani was dying to join.

Miranda slowed to make the turn onto the rutted dirt road leading to her temporary home. A drab brown truck sat in front of the cabin. *Great. Exactly what she needed, a visit from the high command.* It was a two-hour round-trip from Denver to her assigned area, yet Frank Jarrell showed up at least twice a week. She knew it was more than dedication to duty that brought him. He was like a bulldog sometimes. Or a different kind of dog.

She'd been struck by his resemblance to a basset hound the first time they met, thanks to his jeweled face, short, but thick stature and his dark eyes. His gravelly voice and slow way of moving only reinforced that mental image.

"Good afternoon, Frank." Miranda kept her tone neutral as she greeted her supervisor. She was excellent at playing nice.

"Hope you don't mind my stopping by," he said. "I was in the vicinity and decided to see how things are going."

Which, Miranda knew, was code for "have you failed yet?" She was the first female wildlife specialist to work for Frank. Only two years from retirement, she suspected he feared having a woman here instead of a good old boy with a farmer's tan might put a bump in his ride to that golden government pension.

"Actually, it was a good day." She held up her clipboard so he could see the many filled pages. "I met several ranchers, including the one who's running the Hallowell place now."

"Excellent." Frank nodded. "Getting familiar with these people is important. Remember, while you're in that uniform, you represent the entire department."

He gestured toward the porch. "Care if I sit?"

Yes, she most definitely did. The last thing she wanted or needed was a prolonged conversation with her boss. She wanted to kick off her boots, pour herself a glass of something cold and replay what happened back there on the road. She wanted to analyze that encounter with Rik the way she did her findings, to see if she'd missed something in that brief conversation.

Like whether he actually was glad to see her or if he'd have been happier if she'd stayed far away from his ranch.

"You know the government's been asking the ranchers throughout the region to sign new grazing contracts," Frank said after he settled himself on the porch swing, which had seen better days. Miranda took a section of porch rail and nodded.

"The big guys all signed, no problem," Frank said. "Some of the smaller ranches aren't all that happy and they're holding out. They figure since they pay taxes, the land should be available to anyone and everyone for free. I'd like to nip it in the bud."

"Want me to meet with them?"

Frank shook his head. "Eventually. I'm calling some ranchers who see the advantage of guaranteed grazing rights to ask if they'll help. When we have public meetings, I'll be

asking you to be our voice since you're familiar with their land."

Stopping the swing, he leaned forward.

"I'd like you to get to know the folks around here. Sit down and have coffee, build a social life. Let them see we're no threat to their operation. Your job calls for a jack of all trades."

Miranda nodded, looking for a diplomatic way to tell Frank she was no novice at the public relations side of this job.

"I've been talking to people whose ranches intersect the grazing land here on the east," she said, "and they've all been pleasant. I've even been invited in for coffee by several of them."

"You've only scratched the surface," Frank warned. "Some of those old-timers resent any sort of government involvement. You gotta find a way to make them trust you. Getting them on your side is the first step in getting things done."

Leaning back, he abruptly changed the conversation.

"By the way, I wondered how your little girl is back in Michigan without her mama."

Now Miranda knew why he'd come.

"She's doing great, healing fast and ready to get back on a pony anytime."

Disappointment flitted across Frank's face. Miranda hid a smile. He'd urged her to head home after Brittani fell and sprained her wrist. Miranda wasn't surprised when he tried again.

"It must be hard to be away from your child, being a single mother and all," he said. "If you need to go home at any time, please let me know. One phone call and Derek can take your place."

*And I'll be stuck in his.* Frank's pet would be doing the fieldwork she loved, while she was reassigned to data entry and leading guided tours of federal properties. No way was she letting that happen. Her goal was a management position, not a lateral move. "I wouldn't dream of interrupting Brittani's vacation." She offered the best smile she could muster. "My parents wouldn't forgive me either. They're so excited about having her for the whole summer."

After a few more moments of stilted conversation, Frank finally drove away, leaving Miranda alone to finish her reports and deal with the shock of seeing Rikky again. Rik, she reminded herself. Different guy now, not the one she'd loved.

The image returned unbidden of Rik turning away to take the phone call, his jeans riding low on his narrow hips and his sweat-soaked tee clinging to a well-muscled chest. He was a billboard cowboy come to life, and nothing but trouble for her. She'd be damned if she'd let him ruin her life again.

Sighing, she forced her mind away from what once had happened the one time she let her emotions control her common sense. She was a grown woman. She had responsibilities, including a daughter she loved and missed, and who expected to hear from her before she went to bed.

Miranda popped open her laptop and logged on. In a cheerful, breezy style, she told Brittani about the animals she'd seen today and the beautiful sunset of the night before. She ended with the usual "I love you, baby" and a reminder that she'd call on Sunday.

What she didn't tell her daughter was that when she came back after Labor Day, they were going on a special shopping trip–an exploration to buy a house of their very own. The small two-bedroom apartment where they lived was better than staying with her parents, as they had until Miranda finished college and found this position. She wanted more for Brittani and herself. She wanted a house with room for Brittani's friends to sleep over and a yard large enough to get the puppy her daughter kept hinting for.

She smiled as she hit the send button and closed the laptop. She could put up with Frank, Rik and whatever else Colorado threw her way for her own piece of the American Dream.

Chapter Two

"Your supper's in the oven. See you in the morning."

Heeding her warning, Rik stepped back before getting knocked down as Rosie Williman barreled toward the kitchen door. The family's longtime housekeeper was more family than hired help. Rik suspected she was also his mother's spy. No way would Mom have agreed to go help Aunt Lou without reports from back home. He loved his mother, he really did, but she had to know what was going on in everyone's life. The timing of her rare visits to San Francisco had made him wonder more than once if she kept a private detective on retainer. Either that, or ESP told her exactly when to interfere in his life.

"Don't do the dishes," Rosie called as she hurried toward the door. "I'll get them in the morning. You've done enough work for one day."

Rik raised his hand in goodbye, but she was already out the door. Even though she was in her 60s, she was a dynamo. It seemed like if there was a committee formed, she was on it; if a project needed organizing, she was among the first to volunteer. And, as he and his brother had experienced more than once, she also was quick to offer advice, whether it was wanted or not.

Tonight was Thursday and the weekly meeting of the Armont Ladies Civic Improvement League, which explained the basket on Rosie's arm. Supposedly the league's purpose was to improve greater Armont, but over the years their gatherings had also become a cooking competition.

The scent of his own meal drew Rik to the kitchen. He pulled a pan from the stove, pushed up the foil covering and sniffed appreciatively. Pork chops baked with apples and onions, and lots of them—Rosie knew what he liked. He filled his plate and grabbed a beer from the refrigerator, where he discovered a lemon icebox cake for dessert.

Rik settled down on the family room couch and clicked on the television. His mother would be appalled to see him. She was a stickler for family meals around the table and perfectly executed manners. He liked eating as a bachelor again, especially with no pointed hints on producing an heir to the empire thrown into the dinner-time conversation. Mom had never addressed the subject with him until after Ron's abrupt and apparently permanent departure. Now she and Rosie were tag-teaming him in nagging about finding a nice girl and settling down.

He'd almost finished his second chop when the phone rang. Speak of the devil, he thought as he heard his mother's voice on the other end.

"Am I interrupting something?"

She delivered the question in a tone that held expectation. Like maybe she'd dragged him away from baby making or a marriage proposal.

"Finishing supper. I worked on fences today and got in later than I expected."

"Oh."

That single syllable held a world of disappointment, so Rik added, "I was thinking about going to the Cattleman's Club later, though."

"Oh."

Disapproval this time. His mother declared the place vulgar, but she remembered the Cattleman's as a men-only club and the scandalous talk about what went on there. Now it was simply a bar and grill, open to anyone.

"Although I think I'll probably stay home and turn in early," Rik continued. "I'm pretty beat, and I've got more fences to check in the morning. By the looks of them, there hasn't been much maintenance done."

"Your brother did the best he could. He took your daddy's death so hard I wonder sometimes if he'll ever be able to be happy again."

Naturally, his mother jumped to Ron's defense. His younger sibling had always been her favorite. Rik grew up knowing that, and so did Ron. They'd gotten along, two brothers three years apart in age, although everyone knew his father expected Rik to take over the ranch.

"How's Aunt Lou?" Time to change the subject.

"Getting better, but her progress is slow."

The blow-by-blow description of his aunt's recovery took up the rest of the call. Rik only half-listened, his mind occupied with other matters. Like finding the time to do a financial audit of the ranch records. Remembering to order calf feed in the morning. Trying not to think about what a beautiful woman Miranda had become.

"Rik, are you listening to me?"

"Uh, sorry, dropped the phone."

"Well, this is important." A familiar sharpness crept into in his mother's voice. "I've decided to extend my stay. I'm the only sister Lou has, and she needs me. It may be fall before I feel comfortable leaving her."

"Then stay," Rik said. "All you'll do here is worry."

The complacency in Mom's voice pleased him. He knew his mother missed her native Virginia, even after forty years away. The change in scenery and companionship of her siblings might help her recover from losing Dad last winter.

Dinner and conversation finished, Rik considered his options for the evening. He could go to the Cattleman's and hang with the guys for a while. If he took a shower. If he had enough energy to get involved in pool or poker.

If he was willing to let his truck be seen in the parking lot.

The Ladies League met in the church hall across the street from the Cattleman's. Every man in town knew every woman in the league checked to see who was hanging out there.

Rik had learned about the league the hard way, when one eligible woman after another ended up next to him in the pew at church on Sunday.

After a few weeks of the phenomenon, he'd gotten suspicious. A little asking around, and he learned that the Ladies League was as famous for its matchmaking as its food. He decided to stay home tonight. If he lay low, the ladies might set their sights on some other unattached sap who happened to cross their line of vision.

Sighing, he switched off the TV and grabbed his laptop. His work as a ranch hand might be over for the day, but he had a feeling there was plenty waiting in his Domino e-mail box, organized for his inspection by his assistant.

****

In the church hall, Rosie and her serving companion compared notes over coffee and cookies at the refreshment table. Rik had proved a challenge for them ever since his return. Rosie had promised Liz Hallowell she'd make getting Rik hooked up a top priority, and she always kept her promises.

"We're running out of women," Hazel Brown said as she snagged another Mexican wedding cookie. "He's been polite, sharing a hymn book and all, but he's never asked a single one of them out. Not even called, and I've talked to every one of those girls myself."

Rosie sighed. "Armont's a small town," she said. "But I'm not giving up yet. Somewhere out there is the perfect girl for him."

Silence followed as the two conspirators considered the pool of single females.

"There's that new woman out at the cabin," Hazel finally suggested.

"The government girl? She's not his type. His girlfriends have always been dark-haired and busty, the clinging vine type that makes a man feel manly."

"Well, maybe his tastes have changed," Hazel retorted. "That Junie's got an hourglass figure and big bedroom eyes and your Rik never gave her a second look. Maggie made him brownies with her number on top in icing, and he didn't even bother to write it down. Could be he likes independent girls who think like a man."

"But we're taking a big chance," Rosie cautioned. "Even if he takes to her, there's no guarantee she'll want to settle down here. The idea is to give him a reason to stay, after all."

Hazel studied her best friend.

"You're worried the boys will sell the place, aren't you?"

Rosie nodded. "That would be dreadful. Not only because I've been with the Hallowells for years, but because their dad wanted the ranch to be their legacy. Ron's already walked away. If Rik does too, I'm afraid one of those corporate farms will buy the place from their mother and this community will be the poorer for it."

The end of the business meeting and a flood of Ladies Leaguers at the refreshment table postponed the conversation. Hazel picked it back up as the two women cleared the dishes later.

"That girl's all alone out there, in that cabin they gave her to live in. Poor thing probably eats off a hot plate. If I were you, I'd drive out there, invite her to dinner and not tell Rik. He's got enough manners to sit through a meal and make polite conversation, doesn't he?"

So it was settled. Twenty minutes later, Rosie's mini-van was parked by Miranda's cabin, and the housekeeper was sitting on the porch making small talk with what could be her last chance at a fix-up for Rik.

\*\*\*\*

Miranda's first impulse on seeing a strange vehicle pull up after dark was to grab her cell phone and go outside. She wasn't afraid to be here alone, but she was cautious. Keeping Frank's warning about old-line ranchers who resented the government controls on grazing land in mind, she liked being able to call 911 if things got ugly.

"I hope you don't mind a visitor this late in the evening," said the middle-aged woman who climbed out of a minivan with a basket in her hand. "I've been meaning to come welcome you to Armont ever since you moved in, but I haven't found a moment until now."

The woman started up the steps, then stopped and pressed a hand to her chest.

"Just look at me, acting as if we're old friends," she said with a shake of her head, "and you not knowing me from Adam. Well, I'm Rosie Williman and I live on the ranch over there."

She waved her hand in a circle; as far as Miranda could tell, the place was somewhere between Canada and the Pacific Ocean. Not that she cared. Getting a visitor not only made her feel a little less alone, but it also reinforced what she'd told Frank: She was starting to fit in.

"We had so many treats at the Ladies League meeting tonight and I sure don't need to be taking them home," Rosie said, patting her round tummy. "I 'spect you haven't had homemade cookies in a while, so I decided to bring them while they're still fresh."

"Come up on the porch," Miranda invited. "I'll get a dish for them so you can take the basket back with you."

"No need." Rosie handed over the basket and sat down on the swing. "You can bring it tomorrow night when you come for dinner. I imagine you're about ready for a home cooked meal, too. How does pot roast sound?"

Pot roast sounded heavenly after all the quick sandwiches and microwave meals Miranda had been eating. Her mother was a wonderful cook, and Brittani's recitations of what Grandma had fixed for supper had her longing for comfort foods.

"One of my favorites," she confessed.

"Well, good." Rosie beamed at her. "Frank Jarrell tells me you're a single girl, working here for the summer. Tell you the truth, I can't believe Frank hasn't found a way to chase you off yet. He's from the generation that believes women belong in the kitchen, not bringing home a paycheck."

"Frank is a little different," Miranda acknowledged, not wanting to say anything that could backfire if it got back to Frank.

"I sure hope that when he finally retires and sets to making a nuisance of himself at his own house, we get someone who cares more about the folks around here than a fancy title and government pension," Rosie said. "But let's not talk about him. Tell me a little about yourself. I can tell you're not from around here."

"Michigan," Miranda answered. That single word brought a slew of questions from Rosie, starting with the Detroit Tigers and their baseball prowess to what got Miranda interested in her line of work.

Forty-five minutes later, Miranda clutched the basket in her hand and waved goodbye to Rosie. The older woman had dashed down directions to her ranch on a sheet of paper and told Miranda dinner was at six p.m.

"We'll see you tomorrow then." Rosie offered a wide smile as she prepared to leave. "Come hungry. I love to cook, but I do hate leftovers."

****

Right on time, Miranda rolled through a set of weathered iron gates, missing the ranch name as she concentrated on not running over a black hound sleeping in the center of the road. She smoothed her skirt as she got out of the car, hoping she'd dressed right. Her wardrobe was mostly khaki shirts and shorts, although she brought a few dressier items just in case.

Tonight she'd chosen a bright broomstick skirt and red tank, adding some bright papier-mâché jewelry she'd picked up on a shopping trip she'd made with Brittani. As she slipped on the bracelet, she remembered Brittani's "That's awesome, Mom" and smiled.

But Brittani was back home, and Miranda was standing at the heavy wooden door of a traditional adobe ranch house. The door swung open before she could knock, and Rosie hustled her inside.

"My, don't you look nice." The housekeeper beamed. "Come on in and get comfortable."

She showed Miranda to a long salon, chattering about what a pleasant evening it was until the one-sided conversation was interrupted by the ding of a timer. Rosie threw up her hands and hurried back out to the hall.

As she exited, she called back to Miranda, "He's in the shower. Had trouble with a cow and smells terrible. Be right back!"

Miranda was left alone and slightly confused in the middle of a room with comfortable furniture and southwestern furnishings. Dark brown club chairs flanked a stone fireplace, and several divans and loveseats were placed for easy conversation. Miranda decided on a club chair, wishing she had a newspaper to read while she waited for Rosie or the mysterious "he" to appear.

Sitting still and doing nothing was hard for her, so Miranda opened a French door and stepped into a garden more reminiscent of the Southeast than Colorado. A bird feeder was mounted on a post a few feet outside the window, and the feathered creatures were gathered for their evening meal. The faint scent of roses tinted the air, and flowering bushes lined small brick walkways.

The peaceful surroundings settled her nerves; a bubble of anticipation replaced the jitters she'd been fighting over dining with strangers. The feeling lasted until she strolled back to the house, into the salon and came face to face with Rik. He looked every bit as surprised as she felt, but his face became blank as he greeted her with "Good evening, Miranda."

She tried for the same control despite the shock that ripped through her. She fought the urge to flee, her hands tightly clasping the skirt fabric at her sides. Taking a deep breath and commanding her legs to quit shaking, she drew on her reserve of composure and returned his greeting.

"Rik. What a lovely home you have."

*Neutral language, controlled smile.* Surely she could make it through this one meal with him.

"I'm sorry I wasn't here to greet you." Rik stepped closer, took her hands and dropped a small kiss on her cheek. The mixed scent of his cologne and the hint of soap beneath it reminded her of other, better times.

"Rosie didn't warn me we were having company until I walked in a half hour ago," he continued. "I hope you'll excuse my appearance."

Drool over it was more likely. The man looked fine, from the open-collared, burgundy shirt to snug black jeans and boots. His damp hair curled across his forehead, tempting her to run her fingers through the tendrils to smooth them down the way she used to.

"If I'd known…" Miranda began.

Rik's face tightened. "If you'd known Rosie worked for my family, you wouldn't have come. I'm glad you did. I meant what I said out there on the road. I'm not the man I used to be. Can't we pretend we've just met and go from there?"

Before Miranda could form a reply, Rosie popped her head through the doorway.

"Dinner's ready." she said, wiping her hands on a dish towel. "Rik, show our guest to the dining room."

He led Miranda down a wide hallway and through an arched door into what turned out to be a room large enough for a good-sized party. A linen-covered table stood in the center with candles and fresh flowers as a centerpiece.

She discreetly took in their surroundings as Rik pulled out her chair. Ivory walls, blue damask drapes and artwork displayed on the walls. This room also had a wide fireplace with a mantel; wood lay ready to be lit.

"Rosie's pulled out all the stops," Rik said, a note of surprise in his voice as he helped Miranda with her chair before taking the end seat as his own, putting her on his left. "Trust me, I knew nothing about this."

Savory aromas filled the air from the uncovered dishes of food placed within easy reach.

"I think I have everything." Joining them, Rosie sat down heavily. "Rik, will you do the honors?"

The first dish had barely left his hand when Rosie jumped up.

"Salt and pepper!" She took off toward the kitchen, bringing a wide smile to Rik's face.

"You'll get used to her," he said. "I can't remember Rosie ever moving at less than top speed. She's sweet to the bone, and will do anything for you. One warning, though: What Rosie wants, Rosie finds a way to get. My father was one of the strongest-willed men I've known, but even he backed down when Rosie launched a campaign."

"Is she on one now?" Miranda asked.

Rik offered a grim smile. "I suspect my mother has promised her a bonus if she finds a way to keep me here. They both underestimate me. I'm like that stubborn bull that refuses to move."

"Until a pretty heifer comes into the lot." Miranda smiled. "My dad had cattle, remember?"

The conversation ended when Rosie returned, plopping a set of crystal shakers on the table and seating herself. The process of filling plates began again. It was the first home-cooked meal Miranda had enjoyed since she arrived and, despite her nearness to Rik, she soon relaxed.

The conversation was casual and general, much to her relief. The last thing she wanted was to talk about her personal life. The less Rik knew about the last ten years, the happier she'd be.

Rosie proved to be an entertaining dinner companion. She reminded Miranda of her favorite aunt, full of energy and talkative enough for all of them. Between bites, she regaled Miranda with tales of Armont, bringing the small town to life.

The first awkward moment came as Rosie cut the chocolate cake she'd made for dessert. She gave them each a large wedge before bringing a coffee carafe from the kitchen.

"I shouldn't eat this," she said, patting her ample tummy. "But I do love my sweets and it is a celebration of sorts. It's been a long time since we had a beautiful young woman in this house."

"Rosie…" Rik warned.

She forged right ahead. "You know, Miranda, the Civic League is having a pie social at the school gym tomorrow night. You should meet everyone. Ralph Johnson's swing band is going to play and we have door prizes."

"Sounds like fun," Miranda said. Frank's remark about getting to know people resounded in her mind.

"It is," Rosie insisted. "I'll make a nice apple pie for you since you're a working girl. It starts at seven, but most folks come early."

"The school's a couple streets from the post office, right? I'll leave a little early to make sure I find it."

"Oh, Rik can pick you up," Rosie offered, avoiding his eyes.

"No, no, I don't want to impose," Miranda said, panic rising inside her. "I'm sure I can find it. Armont's small."

"This family is known for its hospitality. It won't take ten minutes for Rik to get to your place. I won't hear of you coming all by yourself."

"Honestly, I don't mind."

"Nonsense." Rosie turned to Rik. "Tight as parking can be sometimes, do you see any reason you should both drive?"

Without giving him a chance to answer, she slapped the table, rose and began to clear the plates. "Most of the girls dress up a bit, but you wear whatever is comfy. Nobody in Armont is the least bit fancy."

Miranda knew she was defeated. She also knew there was more than one way to skin a cat. As Rosie started toward the kitchen with the dirty dishes, she said to Rik, "Don't worry about me. I'll drive myself."

He offered a cocky grin. "Are you chicken?"

The bubble of panic inside Miranda erupted into full-fledged dread. She could not, would not, go anywhere with Rik. Not to a pie social or anywhere else.

"Hey, it's all right." Rik laid a hand on her arm in a comforting gesture. When his expression tightened she knew her face must have given away her emotions. "Everyone goes, and lots of folks ride together. Don't make more of this than it is."

"Which would be?" Miranda asked, her voice low and tense.

"Two people sitting on separate sides of the car for fifteen minutes. That's all. Not a date, certainly not picking up on what used to be."

Miranda dropped her head in her hands. What used to be…love and heartbreak, broken promises and consequences she couldn't have imagined.

"Okay," she said, raising her head to meet his eyes. "Fine." She pushed back her chair and stood. "Now I believe I'll find Rosie and say goodbye."

She was grateful Rik didn't follow her down the long hallway, and even more grateful Rosie walked out to the car with her for a final good night. The less time she spent with Rik Hallowell, the safer her heart was…and the secret she'd kept from him all these years.

## Chapter Three

Blouses, skirts, jeans and tees littered her bed by the time Miranda changed clothes for the last time. Still uncertain, she took a last look at herself in the cracked mirror above the dresser.

"Looking good, sister," she said aloud, as if hearing the words would prop up her shaky confidence. Being a stranger was bad enough. The last thing she needed was to stand out like a sore thumb.

Back home, matching clothes to events was easy. Not only was a pie social something new but she didn't know what the occasion demanded. Jeans seemed too casual, the one little black dress she'd bought too dressy. She hoped her teal jersey top and black mid-calf skirt were appropriate. To dress up the outfit, she'd added a wide belt and strapped on low-heeled sandals.

Miranda braided her hair into a thick plait that fell down her back. One more peek in the mirror and she quit looking. She'd fussed enough.

A quick glance at the clock and she realized she was actually early. She called her parents' number and left a cheerful message for Brittani before remembering they'd headed to a strawberry festival for the weekend. She'd hear about that soon enough. One of the last things she'd done before leaving for Colorado was to buy her daughter an inexpensive digital camera so they could e-mail photos back and forth. Living her daughter's adventures vicariously helped them both feel connected.

She took a deep breath when she heard Rik's car on the gravel outside. She listened with trepidation to the snap of boots on the wooden steps and was at the door before Rik had time to knock.

"Hi." She grabbed her purse and scooted out. "You're prompt."

"That's a virtue, right?" Rik smiled at her as they walked down the steps together. "You know, like godliness and cleanliness."

"A small one. More like cleaning your plate and hanging up your jacket."

Before the conversation could turn into full-fledged banter–date-like banter–Miranda opened her car door and hopped in before he could get to her. She set her purse between them, a tactful reminder that this was definitely not a date.

The school gymnasium in downtown Armont blazed with lights when they arrived ten minutes later. Rik led the way to the side entrance, leading her past the tables where pies were set out for inspection.

"How does this work?" Miranda glanced over the large selection and forgot she intended to be aloof.

"The ladies bring pies," Rik explained, "each of which gets a number. The auctioneer starts the bidding among the men. The guy with the highest bid gets the pie and shares it with the woman who baked it."

"Even if it's someone else's wife?"

Rik grinned. "That's the fun of it. There's always some joker who runs a bid way up to make a husband pay."

Miranda laughed. This might be more fun than she expected. And sharing pie with a stranger should help her get to know people, as Frank had ordered.

"You made it!" Rosie came bouncing over, her cheeks flushed from her frantic activity. "Did you see all the pies? This is going to be our best social ever." She looked around, her eyes darting here and there, before confiding, "I put your name on the pie with the red ribbon around it. I thought if I kept it simple, *someone* ought to know which one to buy."

She winked at Rik before scurrying off to find Hazel. When a couple standing near them smiled, Miranda knew Rosie had been overheard. The last thing she wanted or needed was for the people of Armont to think they were a couple.

She sidled away from Rik, looking for an open seat. One open seat, so he would have to sit somewhere else.

"I'll bet you're thirsty." Rik headed toward the punch table without waiting for an answer.

"Really, I'm fine." *Or I would be if I could find a polite way to ditch him.*

Before she came up with one, he was back, a middle-aged couple in tow. They proved to be her escape, leading her around the room to introduce her to practically everyone in town, she suspected. Her head soon reeled from a vain attempt to remember names and faces, and she was very glad when Hazel's voice crackled over the loudspeaker to announce that the auction was about to begin.

"Rosie said blue ribbon, right?" Rik was back, whispering in her ear. He slid his arm around her waist; she immediately pulled away. She kept distance between them as the first pies were bid off. Some sold quickly while others went after a furious round of competitive bidding. Soon the auctioneer, who called for an opening bid, held up the pie with the red ribbon.

"One hundred dollars." Rik's voice soared out. A gasp went up; the most any had brought before was less than half that.

"You gonna let him get away with that?" the auctioneer asked. "The money's going for charity, remember."

"I'll go a hundred and a penny,"came a voice from the back of the room. Laughter greeted his bid.

"One hundred fifty!" Rik shouted, sliding an arm around Miranda's waist.

"I believe we'll declare this one sold," the auctioneer shouted as laughter swelled again. "A man who'd offer that much isn't going to let anyone beat him. Bet you can guess who made this one, can't you?"

Applause filled the room as Rosie motioned for Miranda to acknowledge that it was indeed her pie. Rik strode up to the dais and claimed his prize, holding it in triumph over his head as he came back to clasp Miranda's hand and lead her to an empty spot at one of the long tables.

Rosie moved in with disposable plates and forks, cutting the pie with the side of a silver server and sliding pieces onto two plates. "Eat hearty," she said. "It's your favorite, Rik—lots of nutmeg and extra cinnamon."

She raced off to assist the next pie bidder, leaving them to their dessert. Aware of the stares coming their way, Miranda had no choice but to make the best of things.

"You could have been a little less obvious." Miranda cut off a bite of pie and popped it in her mouth. Even in her stressed-out state, she appreciated its light, fluffy crust and a filling that was both spicy and sweet.

"You knew I was going to buy the pie, they knew I was going to buy the pie, and a hundred fifty is a fair donation," he replied, a smug smile decorating his face.

"If all you wanted to do was help out, you could have bought Mrs. McAllister's pie," Miranda retorted. "A nice widow lady like that must make good pie, and she'd be thrilled to have a good-looking man like you sitting next to her."

"So you think I'm good-looking, huh?" Rik grinned and raised an eyebrow. "In an unattainable god sort of way, or the rugged mountain man kind?"

"You are incorrigible, did you know that? Mark this night on your calendar, because it's the last time I'm paying you anything even remotely like a compliment."

Any response from Rik was stopped by the arrival of the Methodist minister and his wife. The good reverend was nearly as round as he was tall, and his wife was equally rotund. They were kind, friendly folks, however, and Rik greeted them warmly.

Others came up to tease Rik, asking if the pie was worth a hundred fifty dollars. Miranda slipped away to refill her punch cup, content to let the conversation flow around her. She was having a much better time than she'd expected despite Rik's constant presence. She told herself she was relieved when a busty brunette grabbed Rik's arm and stood on her tiptoes to kiss his cheek. An old flame? A new flame?

Not that it was any of her business.

"Ralph's almost ready." Rosie stopped and patted Miranda's shoulder. "He's good, Miranda, so I hope you know how to two-step."

"I claim the first dance."

She started at Rik's voice behind her. Rosie grabbed the pie pan from his hand, promising to keep the leftovers safe. "I don't feel like dancing," Miranda lied. "It's warm in here and I'm sort of sleepy after eating that pie. A little air will probably help."

She cut through the crowd, heading toward the makeshift dance floor in the center of the gym, her steps quick. She needed to get away from the crowd and from Rik before their not-a-date changed into one. Rosie's meddling reinforced what Rik had said: the woman was

The cool breeze cleared Miranda's head as she took a deep breath of clean air. The sky was clear as far as the eye could see; a field of stars twinkling down at her, courtiers to the huge, full moon.

Wandering to the playground equipment, she sat down on a wooden swing and wrapped her hands around the heavy metal chains. Closing her eyes, she let solitude wash over her.

"You okay?" came a deep, familiar voice.

She opened her eyes. Rik leaned against the metal leg of the swing set, watching her.

"Fine. Just thinking."

"About?"

"The complexities of being a grown-up."

"Hold on and I'll help you forget."

Before she could stop him, he grabbed the chains, pulled them back and let go to start Miranda on a gentle glide. She pumped with her legs, slowly at first, then going higher and higher. How many years had it been since she'd been on a swing? Since Brittani was tiny? Even before that?

An unexpected exhilaration filled her as she soared back and forth. Her skirt flew up and her hair escaped from the neat braid as she gained momentum. Finally she allowed the swing to slow and she dragged her feet to stop, nearly breathless. The giddy feeling continued as she slid from the swing and ran laughing to the teeter-totter.

"Help me out here," she called as she sat on the low seat." Unless you've forgotten how to do it."

"When it comes to you, Miranda, I haven't forgotten a thing."

Rik's voice was no longer teasing. He pulled her off the wooden seat, clasping her to his body before she could protest. She should have resisted when he bent his head to capture her lips in a long, deep kiss that let her know he hadn't forgotten a single moment from their past.

Her hungry body led her to lean against him, ignoring her common sense. He grasped an escaped curl in his fingers as his tongue sought hers and he pushed against her with the proof of his desire. He was right; they weren't kids anymore. She wanted him, she needed him, and the consequences be damned.

A sudden sweep of headlights as someone left the social broke them apart. Miranda sagged against the swing set for support as her legs wavered uncertainly beneath her.

"I hadn't planned to do that."

Rik's voice was quiet, the remorse in it real.

"I know." She took a deep breath, willing her body to relax. "Me, either. Trouble is, we're still operating on old times. It's been ten years, Rik, and I've changed. You have, too. Let's consider that the goodbye kiss we never had."

Rik turned his face toward the star. "Sure."

He hadn't meant to kiss her. Now that he had, he wanted to kiss her again, and again. He wanted to whisk her to that little cabin of hers, far away from prying eyes and gossiping neighbors, where they could spend the night sating each other.

He wanted to know if she was still ticklish just below her waist, if her breasts were as ripe as he remembered, if she'd call out his name when she climaxed, her nails raking down his naked back. Grateful for the darkness that hid the bulge straining against his fly, he shoved the memories back. Miranda was right about one thing. He wasn't Rikky anymore. The business world had taught him the value of patience and self-control, and he knew how persuasive he could be in the right circumstances. Time, that's all he needed. Time and more ways to be near her.

"I hear music." Miranda nodded toward the gym's lit windows. "Why don't we go listen to the band?"

"All the single men will want to dance with you."

"They'll be disappointed. I don't dance."

"No waltzing?" he asked in mock amazement as they walked back to the building. "Or the cotton-eyed Joe? And you call yourself an American?"

She laughed. "My mother spent enough time and money sending to me to ballet classes to prove I have no aptitude for dance. Besides there wasn't much chance to dance at my high school."

"Oh, that's right," Rik said. "You went to a private school, didn't you?"

"My parents decided I'd do well in an all-girls school. They insisted it was for the academic advantage, but I figured it was because dating was frowned upon so it couldn't interfere with our grade point average. I never went to a football game, let alone homecoming or the prom."

"You poor thing. Such a deprived childhood. Let me make it up to you. The first time Ralph starts calling a square dance, I'll teach you to promenade and do-si-do."

****

True to his word, Rik rounded up six others and formed a square when the bandleader started calling out commands to a Blake Shelton tune. The steps were simple, and the others went out of their way to help her, but Miranda still ended up in the wrong place and with the wrong partner at song's end. She bowed to her partner, as the caller instructed, before escaping to an empty chair, her face warm from exertion and her hair straggling around her neck.

Rik offered her a cup of punch.

"Here's your reward for a valiant try."

"You need to offer it to everyone else as a consolation prize." She fanned her face with her free hand and took a sip. The punch had warmed since the pie sale, but it was liquid and she was parched.

She watched from the sidelines the rest of the evening, declining offers to dance from various men who had come stag. When the building began to empty as the band swung into the final song of the evening, Miranda stood as Rik came toward her.

"Ready to go?" he asked.

"I thought I'd see if they need help in the kitchen cleaning up," she answered. "Go on. I'm sure Rosie will take me home."

"Chicken to get in the car with me?" His voice teased but his gaze was serious. She suspected he remembered their kiss.

She arched an eyebrow, refusing to take the bait.

"I'll let you eat pie out of the pan all the way to your place."

She tried to hide her smile but failed.

"You can explain the intricacies of ballet now that I've taught you all about square dancing."

"Enough already. Let's go." Laughter underscored her words.

Rik crossed the room with her as she said goodbye to Rosie and the others she'd met during the social. The parking lot was thinning out as they drove away from the school and out of Armont. Rik fiddled with the radio until classic rock filled the car.

"Did you enjoy yourself?" he finally asked.

"I did." Miranda smiled in the dark. "I didn't know what to expect, but it was fun."

Being with Rik made this memorable. There were traces of the young rancher's son she first met still evident in the man he'd grown into. He was confident but not cocky, at ease but not condescending. If she were shopping for someone special in her life, Rik would be exactly the kind of man she'd want to see again.

Unfortunately, there was no way to erase the past. They shared a history that had caused her too many tears and too much heartache. Her new life didn't have a place for him. Her first concern was Brittani and creating a good future for them both.

"Home again, safe and sound." Rik cut the engine as he pulled up to the cabin. "Want me to go in first and check for snakes?"

Miranda laughed. "I'm pretty sure it's snake-free."

"Coyotes?"

"No coyotes, either, and no wolves." She yawned. "All that's waiting is my bed. I'm ready to snuggle in and sleep forever."

"I guess it's good night then."

"I guess it is." Miranda reached for the door handle.

"So good night."

"Good night."

Rik leaned toward her, but she pulled the handle and slipped out before he could kiss her. Twice in one night was more than she could handle.

She slid into bed a few minutes later, punched the pillow and closed her eyes. A half-hour later, she was still trying to sleep. Every time she closed her eyes, she saw Rik's image and her awakened body remembered what was supposed to follow a kiss like theirs. Finally, she gave up, got up and grabbed her checkbook.

Balancing her account had always been her sure-fire cure for insomnia. Now she'd see if it was as effective in blotting out the memories of a man.

Chapter Four

*A familiar song played from the clock radio next to the bed as Randi snuggled against Rikky's naked body. He wrapped an arm around her, pulling her tightly against him without waking. She cuddled her face against his chest and breathed in the scent of him. Being with Rikky seemed so right and the life he promised possible.*

*She'd never slept with a guy before, although her friends were sure she had. They thought she did it with Brian. After all, they'd been dating for months and Brian was a guy no sane girl said no to. Everyone knew that. Brian probably bragged to his own friends about things they'd never done, but she didn't care. As her mother reminded her all the time, "be true to yourself" was a credo to live by.*

*Being true to herself meant waiting for the right guy. For Rikky. He was sweet and sexy, smart and determined. He was her soul mate, and they'd be together forever.*

In her dream, a teenaged Miranda wakened Rik with teasing kisses along his jaw line and down his neck. She giggled as he awoke and growled at her even as his hands stroked down her body and awakened all the need she thought had already been quenched. Sighing, she settled on her back as Rikky rolled on top, settling between her thighs and kissing her until she thought she'd go crazy.

*"I love you," Rikky whispered as he slid inside and Randi wrapped her legs around him. "Forever. Longer than forever. Until the world ends and the stars explode."*

Miranda woke with a start, her breasts aching, her body damp with sweat and desire. She quit having that dream a long time ago. She'd left it behind with her foolish, girlish belief in soul mates and destiny. That she'd not only had it again but remembered every detail was a bad omen.

She threw off the covers and walked out to the porch. Stars twinkled above and a half-moon illuminated the night sky. Maybe four o'clock. Too early to get up. Going back to bed wasn't an option. Sleep might mean sliding back into the dream, and she didn't want to relive that time with Rik again. Didn't want to remember his kisses, and how no one else had made her feel that way. Not even once in ten long years.

Padding back into the house, she sought the couch. She opened her laptop and brought up a horror movie, one she'd wanted to see but had forbidden Brittani to watch. That ought to keep her awake.

She woke slowly to sunlight streaming in the window and a blank computer screen. If she dreamed, she didn't remember doing so. She did, however, have a headache and a kink in her neck from sleeping without a pillow. She struggled up, trying to decide whether to seek the solace of her bed or give in and stay up for the day.

Fingers pressed to her temples, attempting a drug-free headache reliever she'd read in a magazine, she didn't hear a car pull up or footsteps on the porch. When a voice called, "Good morning, dear," she jumped and gave a shriek.

"Oh, my, did I startle you?" Rosie apologized as she stepped inside the cabin. "I shouldn't have walked in like I did. I'm out of the habit of knocking, I'm afraid. No one's a stranger in Armont."

"Don't worry about it." Miranda was relieved it was only Rosie and not the man who had populated her dreams. "I'm still half asleep, I guess."

Rosie settled on the edge of the worn loveseat and reached into the oversized tote bag she carried.

"I got to thinking that you probably don't eat too good, living out here all by yourself, so I brought you some chicken and dressing. Made it fresh and stuck it in the oven while I was at church." She handed over a lidded plastic dish. "I also wondered if you're free for dinner tonight."

"I'd love to come, but this is the only day I have to do housework," Miranda hedged. She didn't want to hurt Rosie's feelings, yet she was more certain than ever that exposure to Rik wasn't a good thing.

"Don't tell me you have to clean!" Rosie glanced around the spotless room. "It's Sunday, a day of rest. You shouldn't be working."

"I've got laundry to do," Miranda said. "Uniforms, towels, quite a bit actually."

"Which will get much cleaner in the washer at the ranch than at the coin laundry. Pack your clothes up and bring it with you. We're neighborly around here."

Rosie stood and grabbed her bag. "Well, that's settled. Come around six and bring your appetite. Rik's cooking ribs on the barbecue tonight."

Miranda waited until nearly four o'clock to call the ranch and plead a headache. She felt a teensy bit guilty, since she'd killed the headache with two aspirin and Rosie's food, but she didn't exactly tell a lie. She'd awakened with one, after all, and who knew when it might come back?

Rosie was all clucking sympathy, insisting she knew the perfect way to cure a headache.

"Ask anyone and they'll tell you all it takes is a strong cup of my chicory coffee and a chocolate bar," she said. "I'll brew up that coffee and send Rik on out with it. I've got potato salad to make or I'd bring it myself."

Miranda knew when she was beaten. The fates hated her.

"Maybe if I take something I'll feel better," she said, conceding defeat. "I've got a couple of hours yet."

"That's my girl," Rosie said, with enough triumph in her voice to convince Miranda she'd seen through the lie. "You sure you feel up to driving?"

"Positive." Miranda definitely wanted her wheels there as a means of escape. "See you at six."

****

She wasn't at all surprised when Rik opened the door before she knocked.

"I'm so glad you could make it." His voice was warm and as tempting as melted honey on a hot biscuit. "The ribs are ready but Rosie says she's running a little behind, so we should entertain ourselves until the rest of the food is done."

Miranda suspected Rosie's delay was an excuse to make sure she and Rik spent time alone. Unfortunately, there was nothing she could do to prove it short of marching into the kitchen and lifting lids off pots. Following Rik into the salon, she declined a drink. She waited as he poured himself a glass of straight Kentucky bourbon.

"We could walk in Mom's garden," he suggested.

"My headache," she said, waving a hand in the general area of her face. "The pollen might make it worse."

She expected him to laugh or at least raise an eyebrow. He didn't.

"I'm afraid this is going to be a short evening," she said, even though he hadn't responded. "I hate to eat and run, but…"

"But you're going to eat and run."

Time to change the topic, she decided.

"Are you getting the ranch back in order?" she asked, taking a seat on the settee.

Rik shrugged. "Not really. I've managed to get a lot done, but when I get one problem fixed, three more seem to pop up. Once I get a handle on things, I intend to hire a couple of men to help. But I am getting used to being here again. How are you settling in?"

*Dang it, he shifted the conversation back to her.*

"As well as one can in temporary quarters." She shrugged. "I can survive most anywhere, but there really is no place like home."

"Do your parents still have their dairy farm?"

Miranda laughed. "It's nothing more than forty acres and a couple of cows. The farm is only a hobby for Dad, since he's a corporate tax attorney. He still raises purebred Jerseys, although he quit showing them after I moved away."

"Ah, you're part of mobile America, then."

The statement sounded like a question, one she didn't intend to answer. Her address was one of the many things he didn't need to know.

"The food's ready." Rosie popped her head in to make the announcement that dinner was on the table. Miranda hurried into the dining room before Rik could offer his arm, determined to get this meal over with and retreat back to her own, temptation-free place.

To her great relief, the dinner conversation was mostly an impersonal rehash of the pie social. She relaxed and joined in, laughing at Rosie's stories of the Morrison girl's runny blueberry pie and the way old Mrs. McAllister made every single man in the room dance with her at least once.

Still, as soon as good manners permitted, Miranda said her goodbyes. She'd barely driven twenty feet toward freedom when she heard the telltale thumping of a bad tire and, with a groan, shut off the vehicle. She jumped out of the car hoping she was wrong. Instead she came face to tread with the offending tire, flat as a pancake. Sighing, she opened the trunk and lifted the cover to the compartment where the spare was stored. Or would be, if she had one. The empty trunk didn't hold a baby tire or even a jack.

Miranda weighed her options, which ran from slim to none. No way could she make it home without ruining both the tire and the rim. And it was Sunday night in Armont, where service from its one and only garage was strictly a Monday through Friday, nine to five thing.

"Something wrong?"

She stifled a groan. Rik, ever the gentleman, was coming to check on her.

"I've got a flat and the spare is missing," she said. "I guess I should have checked before now."

Rik bent down and ran his hand across the tire. Straightening, he said, "I don't feel anything in it. I've got an air compressor. Maybe it will hold enough air to get you home tonight and back into town tomorrow."

Ten minutes later, after he'd removed his dress shirt, pulled off the tire and examined it under a flashlight's beam, Rik gave Miranda the bad news.

"It's shot." He leaned the rim against the vehicle. "Tomorrow, I'll go into town to get a new one. It won't take long to get you going once there's a new tire on that wheel."

Every word Rik said made sense, but the more he said, the deeper her dread.

"I hate to ask, but can you run me home?" she asked.

Rik leaned against the car and folded his arms across his chest, as if he was thinking.

"I don't like to drive when I've been drinking," he said. "Why don't you stay here? We've got plenty of room." A half-smile crossed his face. "Unless there's some reason you don't want to spend the night."

*You.*

Miranda suspected, as Rik's smile widened, that he knew the answer. She wasn't about to confirm it, though.

"That does make sense, I suppose."

****

Her reluctance bothered Rik more than he liked, although he tried not to let it show. Rosie rushed off to make up a bed. Miranda insisted on going along to help, leaving Rik alone in the kitchen to wash his hands and think.

Could she be afraid of being alone with him?

Maybe. She'd said it herself. They were different people than that they'd been that summer. He learned a lot out on his own, especially how to survive after that break with his father. Yet he'd never found anyone who saw inside him as Miranda had, or made him believe that whatever he dreamed was possible. Those other women been amusing companions and occasional lovers, nothing more, happy to accept the protective armor of light-hearted banter he wore to conceal the real person he hid.

"I'm leaving now." Rosie entered the kitchen. "I'll be here early enough to make you both a good breakfast." She patted Rik's arm. "Don't hesitate to call if you need me."

The air that swept in as Rosie left held a chill, reminding Rik there were no extra blankets in the guest rooms. He found a woven cotton spread in the linen closet and carried it to Miranda's room, gently rapped on the closed door.

Miranda's hair lay in a cloud across her shoulders as she answered his knock, attired in a simple nightgown from his mother's closet. She held a hairbrush in front of her, almost like a weapon, and wore a wary look on her freshly washed face.

"I thought you might need this." He couldn't help staring, even though he knew it was wrong. Lamplight outlined Miranda's body beneath the thin fabric, revealing softer curves than she'd had a decade earlier. The soft billow of her hair made him want to pull her close and bury his face in it. He wanted to lift her up, carry her to his own bed and make love to her.

"Thank you." Miranda took the blanket, her cheeks reddening. Had her thoughts mirrored his?

Wishful thinking, he decided as he forced his eyes away and with a quick muttered good night walked to his own room down the hall. She'd made it plain enough that there wasn't a place for him in her life, not even temporarily.

Inside his bedroom, Rik pulled off his boots before stripping down for a hot shower to wash the grime and car dirt from his body before sliding between the sheets. He'd managed a lot of work over the last few weeks, whittling the must-do list he'd started with to a handful of manageable jobs. Working with his hands again, doing the kind of manual labor where he could see the results immediately, turned out to be more gratifying than he'd expected. He could see himself using the ranch as an escape from his demanding life in San Francisco, maybe even retire back here someday.

"First things first," he reminded himself as he toweled off. When Frank Jarrell asked him to attend the public grazing meetings, he'd agreed for two reasons: because it was what his father would have and done and because he might find a candidate for ranch manager.

****

"Good morning." Rosie's voice reached Miranda as she walked into the kitchen. "You might as well slow down and have some breakfast. Rik's already taken that the tire into town."

The heavenly smells made Rosie's offer impossible to refuse. Thick slices of crisp bacon filled a platter in the center of the table, nestled next to a basket of the fluffiest biscuits Miranda had ever seen. She sat down and poured herself a cup of coffee from the carafe. She barely stirred in the cream before Rosie placed a plate in front of her with a well-filled western omelet.

"Sleep well?" Rosie asked, sitting across from Miranda with her own cup.

"Very well," she lied.

Rosie chuckled. "I guess you always have circles under your eyes when you're well-rested, huh."

"I did wake up off and on," Miranda confessed, unwilling to reveal that every time she woke, her mind turned to Rik. "That happens when I sleep someplace different."

"Me, too." Rosie picked out a biscuit and slathered it with butter and marmalade. She settled back in her chair and eyed Miranda speculatively.

"By now I expect you know I'm a woman to speak my mind," she said. "I don't mean to get personal but I need to know something. Rik's mother and I have been trying to find him a good woman to settle down and have kids with, but he hasn't showed the least interest in anyone until you. You think the two of you might get serious?"

wonder if getting into a little trouble would be such a bad thing after all.

Chapter Five

Miranda managed to keep busy enough over the next few days to keep her mind from returning to Rik and the way he kept cropping up in her life. She headed out early and stayed out until nearly dusk. After a quick dinner, she entered the data from her counts onto a spreadsheet to be e-mailed on Friday to the Denver office.

Thursday was a hot day when every living thing except Miranda herself seemed to find a cool place to hide. Giving up after an hour or two, she headed into Armont. She was ready for a real meal.

A few vehicles sat in the lot at the Cattleman's when she pulled in. None of them, thank goodness, looked like Rik's. Running a hand through her hair, she grabbed her purse and headed into the restaurant. Blessed air conditioning hit her as she walked through the door and spotted an empty booth.

She'd barely gotten settled, hadn't even seen a waitress, when a woman roughly her own age slid into the seat across from her. Miranda recognized her; she was the busty brunette who'd been talking to Rik at the pie social.

"Hi," she said, expecting a simple welcome to Armont as a response.

"Junie Delacroix," said the brunette. "Life-long resident of this town."

"Um, that's nice."

"I'm the third generation of my family to live here."

"Oh, really?"

"My grandmother married a man from here in Armont and my mother married my dad, who also grew up here. Now, as you may have noticed, there's distinct shortage of hot guys here." Junie put her hands on the table, palms down, and leaned toward Miranda. "Rik Hallowell is definitely in that small group, and you need to understand that you're nothing but a summer fling. When he settles down, it will be with someone who has more in common with him."

"Like you."

"Exactly," Junie agreed, straightening up. "We're already dating, you know. Come here on karaoke night and see for yourself."

Miranda wasn't sure if Junie was laying down the law or offering a challenge, but she had no intention of playing her game. She couldn't blame the woman for running after Rik. He was most definitely one of the best-looking men around, and she suspected he had plenty of money without the ranch. If Junie was looking for a different lifestyle than Armont offered, she'd find it wherever Rik was going back to.

"I came to Armont to do my job, and dropped in here for lunch," she said. "No offense, but we're strangers, and I really don't want to talk about your love life, or lack of one."

Junie's face reddened and her hands curled into small fists. Eyes narrowing, she leaned down and said, "Just remember what I said. Hands off Rik."

Shoving away, she stomped as best she could in three-inch sandals toward the juke box in the back. Miranda yanked the menu from behind the napkin dispenser and began to study it as a wailing country ballad began to play. After the waitress took her order for a steak burger and fries, she went back outside, dropped her quarters in the newspaper box and pulled out a paper. She wanted to make sure she had something to concentrate on beside the glares Junie was giving her.

The burger was fat and juicy, delicious enough to make her forget everything but how good it tasted. She ate slowly, enjoying every bite as well as the perfect cup of coffee that went with her meal. When the waitress returned to check on her, she was tempted to order a piece of chocolate cake, but resisted. Too much lunch and she'd want a nap instead of going back to work.

To her relief, Junie was gone by the time she walked up to the register to pay her bill. Armont might be a small town, but she intended to avoid anywhere that woman might be. Unfortunately, avoiding her boss wasn't going to be as easy.

"Good afternoon, Frank," she said as she answered her cell phone.

"I thought you might be out of range but I thought I'd call anyway," he said. "I hope you don't have plans for late afternoon. I'd like to drop by and talk to you about those public grazing meetings. We've gotten the go-ahead."

"Fourish at my place?"

"Four would be fine. I hope you don't mind, but I've invited a rancher to join us. He's very articulate and respected by his peers. I'm sure the two of you will get along fine."

Before she could ask who that might be or even say goodbye, there was nothing but static. Apparently Frank's phone had dropped the call. Sighing, she tucked her own phone in her pocket and headed for her car. This was one of those days that made her wonder why she'd bothered getting out of bed.

The next hours passed quickly as the day began to cool and creatures began to stir. She found a trail near a water source that yielded good results, but she was ready to tuck it in and head for home as four o'clock neared. She wasn't looking forward to listening to Frank pontificate about how generous the government was in granting grazing rights, but with any luck, he'd be in a hurry to get on the road.

She'd changed into capris and a tee by the time she heard a vehicle pull up to the cabin. She stepped out ready to greet her boss and saw Rik walking toward the porch instead.

"Rosie sent leftover meat loaf?" she asked in a light tone.

"Just cookies." He held up a small bag. "Which I suppose we'll have to share with Jarrell though."

Miranda's heart sank. Rik was the rancher Frank had chosen? He was the one she'd be hosting meetings with?

Her panic must have shown on her face because Rik began to smile.

"You don't have to look like I just announced the death squad is on its way," he said. "You've got a few minutes to hide 'em before he shows up."

"Maybe they'll sweeten him up," she said, regaining her composure. "Or take his mind off worrying whether something's going to screw up his last few months on the job. Come on in. I'll put coffee on."

****

A slight swell of victory rose in Rik as he followed Miranda inside. He felt like a warrior invading enemy territory, since she'd made it plain when he picked her up or dropped her off that her living space was off limits. Yet here he was, walking into a room that bore the small touches women used to make even a temporary place a home. A bouquet of wildflowers sprouted out of a glass bottle which served as a centerpiece on a table that had seen better days. A quick glance through the door off the room showed him her bed, covered with a bright quilt.

"I know Frank's a coffee drinker but I also have iced tea if you'd prefer."

Miranda spoke with her back to him, busy measuring coffee into a filter.

"Either one. Whatever's easier."

"Since I rarely make coffee, the tea is probably safer. The coffee pot was here when I moved in, but this is the first I've used it." She turned to smile at Rik. "Frank gets it anyway, good or bad. But I'd hate to make you sick with it."

The tension that had been coiled inside Rik relaxed. Maybe what he took for dismay at his arrival had been simply a manifestation of Miranda freaking about Frank coming to visit. Rik knew what the man said about her. Or rather, what he didn't say. Usually Frank bragged on his staff, but Rik hadn't heard one compliment about Miranda. That was going to change today. Before Frank hightailed it back to Denver, he'd say something nice.

The aroma of coffee filled the cabin by the time Frank walked in and, with a nod to Miranda, greeted Rik enthusiastically. He sat down at the table and nodded yes to Miranda's offer of coffee, adding an ample dose of creamer and sugar until his drink was more beige than brown. He also helped himself to the cookies; Rik made a mental note to tell Rosie they were appreciated.

"So, Frank, how's everything in the big city?" Rik settled back in his chair and stared at the man.

"Just fine. Busy, of course, but I'd rather have too much to do than sit around twiddling my thumbs."

"Apparently Miranda feels the same way. You sent the right person. She's a real hard worker."

"I pride myself on knowing the best man for the job," Frank said, puffing up a little.

"Or in this case, the right woman."

"Yes, yes, the right woman. Now let's talk about how we're going to get folks to our meetings. We need someone besides the malcontents. Miranda, you'd better take notes."

Rik caught the look of aggravation that crossed her face as she stiffened, got up and walked over to the desk a few yards away. He held out his hand for the notebook and pen she retrieved.

"If you two don't care, I'll jot down the basics," he said. "Miranda only has a laptop while I have a full array of equipment at my place. If we're going to start the meetings the end of this week, it will easier to print the materials we need here rather than have it printed up at your office. If you don't object, that is."

Frank's face flushed and his eyes narrowed, but he offered a tight-lipped agreement. Rik wanted to high-five Miranda, but figured he'd rubbed enough salt in the wound already.

"Nice of you to take time to go with our girl here," Frank said as he settled into his chair. "I expect you're a busy man."

"The Hallowell name carries a lot of weight around here," Rick said. "My father's doings, not mine. But as long as I'm here, I'd like to help out. Every ranch around has a stake in what the government does with its land, and I want to have some idea how things set before I get a manager in and go back home."

An hour later, they'd sketched out the basic format for the meetings, decided what towns to meet in and the main talking points for their presentations. The cookies were gone and Frank had gone through three cups of coffee before he stood, hitched up his pants and said, "I need to get going. Call me if anything comes up."

"I will," Rik and Miranda said in unison.

After Frank was out of earshot, Rik said, "So what circumstances would make you call that man for advice?"

"If a meteor wiped out this place maybe," Miranda said with a laugh.

"I was thinking more along the lines of hell freezing over," Rik said with a wry smile. "I don't know what his middle name is, but I think 'Pompous' would suit him fine."

"He does have a lot of experience."

"And a lot of prejudice. I don't like the way he treats you."

Miranda sighed. "You mean like I'm short a few brain cells because I don't have a penis? Don't worry; he's not the only one reviewing my performance. A copy of all my reports go both to Frank and *his* supervisor, so it would be hard for him to completely undermine me. I do feel sorry for his wife, though."

Rik laughed and stood.

"I've got a conference call in about an hour, so I better head home." He handed her a card from his back pocket. "This has my e-mail and cell phone. Can you forward me that document Frank was talking about?"

"Sure."

"I'll get the agenda and other stuff to you by noon tomorrow. If you have any questions before Thursday's public meeting, just give me a call."

Miranda was relieved to see the back of Rik. How had she ended up with the two men most likely to affect her future right here, at the same time? Sheer bad luck, she hoped. If the fates had set something in motion, she didn't want to know anything about it.

When she first met Rik, she still believed in soul mates and destiny. That was before reality taught her a harsh lesson; hard work is what's needed to create a good life, not the perfect alignment of the stars or some goddess pulling strings, like the ancients believed. Despite knowing Frank had it in for her, Miranda had considered it an honor to be the government representative until she realized she'd be the one held to the fire if things went wrong. Still, being given a cash bonus for each meeting served as incentive for her to hang in there. Brittani was going to need braces soon, and their dental plan wouldn't cover it all. She could endure anything for her child.

**** 

The sound of a motor cut through the silence of the ranch land, irritating Rik who was in the mood for peace and quiet. As the noise grew louder, he realized someone on a four-wheeler was responsible not only for the roar but also the cloud of dust rolling toward him. He dropped onto the seat of his own ATV and waited to see who it was.

The body that eventually unfolded from the stopped four-wheeler was most definitely female, clad in short cutoffs, a tee that clung to her substantial curves and bright red boots.

"Hi, Rik." The greeting came out as a purr.

"Hi, Junie. Are you lost?"

"No, silly," she giggled. "I stopped by your house and Rosie told me you were riding fences out this way. I thought you might be ready for a break."

Without waiting for an answer, she grabbed a soft-sided cooler and unzipped it.

"I hope you're hungry." She sat down and patted the grass beside her. "Cooking's a hobby of mine."

Rik only wanted to get done with his work and get back to the house. In two hours he'd be taking part in a conference call with Domino's European vice-presidents and he had yet to check his e-mail or download the documents he needed. He hadn't factored in time for a leisurely lunch, no matter how tempting the food Junie put on the cloth she'd spread on the ground.

He tamped down his irritation with Junie for showing up and Rosie for telling where he was. No way could anyone else understand the pressure of juggling his corporate duties and his duty to his mother to make sure the ranch could smoothly once he was gone. And the chicken salad croissant Junie handed him looked awfully tempting. He liked Rosie's cooking all right, but he didn't mind a change from time to time.

"This is good," he said after his first bite.

Junie smiled as if she'd just won the lottery.

"I try."

"You succeeded."

"Can I ask you something?" Junie inquired, her shadowed and mascaraed eyes wide as she stared at him.

"Sure."

"There's a karaoke competition at the Cattleman's this Saturday, and I'd like you to be my partner in it. The guys down there said you can sing really well."

Rik laughed. "I gave that up years ago and I'm not about to make a fool of myself."

"Then will you come and cheer me on? There's a $250 prize to the winner, which will just about cover the repairs to my car."

Rik bit off a big bite of croissant, stalling for time as he thought her request through. He wouldn't mind hanging around the Cattleman's, and if word got back to Rosie that he was seen with a local woman, she might ease up on the matchmaking. "Please say yes," Junie begged. "Seriously, I need that money and it's easier for me to sing to one person than a crowd. If you just sit at a table and let me focus on you, I know I can win this thing."

Rik felt a tiny pang of guilt. It had been a long time since such a small sum as $250 had made a difference in his life, but he remembered what it was like to be nearly flat broke and facing trouble. Would it kill him to watch her? No.

"Okay," he finally said. "I'll meet you there before the competition starts."

Junie pressed both hands to her chest.

"Oh, thank you, thank you, thank you. Can I ask one more favor? Since my car's not running, can you pick me up?"

He should have known there was a catch. He'd like to say no, but since he passed her small house on the way into town, he couldn't find an excuse. "See you Saturday then," he said. "About eight?"

"Perfect!" Junie smiled and began to gather up the remnants of their impromptu picnic. "It's a date."

*Which was exactly what he was attempting to avoid.* As he waved goodbye to her, he was already beginning to regret the impulse that had made him say yes.

****

Thursday afternoon was hot and dry, like every day so far that week. While he'd rather make the 90-mile trip to the first grazing rights meeting in the luxury of his sleek sedan, he knew the roads. Some of them would be graveled and rutted and his baby was built for super highways.

He'd dressed the way he expected his fellow ranchers would be, in jeans and a dark blue shirt with a navy tee under it. He'd been surprised when he saw Miranda in dressier clothes until he realized she expected Frank to have a spy in the audience. Frank was fond of looking like a government man; Rik suspected he wanted his staffers to maintain the same appearance.

"You're awfully quiet," he said, glancing over from the driver's seat at Miranda. "You aren't car sick, are you?"

"I'm fine. Enjoying the ride."

Her tone was cool. Rik figured her mood was from emotion and had nothing to do with him. She'd gotten a call soon after they left her place, and although he didn't deliberately eavesdrop, it was hard not to overhear in the pick-up's cab.

"I didn't know you had a kid," he said in an attempt at conversation.

Miranda's tone went to frosty. "There's a whole lot about my personal life you don't know."

"Kinda touchy, aren't you?"

"Some things aren't up for discussion."

"Like whether you've had the tattoo on your ass lasered off yet?"

Miranda gasped.

"That's not a tattoo, it's a birthmark!"

"I'd say it's more like a beauty mark." Rik grinned and raised one eyebrow.

Miranda shot him an if-looks-could-kill stare.

"Maybe you ought to forget about my birthmark and worry about your women," she said.

Rik frowned. What the hell was she talking about?

"I'm not dating anyone."

"So you say."

"Jealous, are you?"

When she didn't bother with a reply, he figured something other than his love life was eating at her. Maybe she was nervous about running the meeting. Or maybe it was PMS. He'd never been good at figuring out women.

After a few minutes of silence, she snapped out, "How much farther?"

"Another twenty miles or so." He glanced down at the odometer. "We've gone seventy, and it's just shy of a hundred if I remember right. Think you can take another half hour?"

"I am absolutely wonderful." She turned her head to stare out the window. "I wanted to spend my day driving to the middle of nowhere in a farm truck with hot air and dust blowing in the windows at me. What excites me the most is that we'll have so many more opportunities to do this whole damn thing again."

Rik turned his head to hide a grin. She'd been prickly all day, with one small gripe after another. His cigarette lighter didn't work, so she couldn't charge her cell phone as they drove. Her hair was a mess, and her clothes would be ruined by the time they got there. The dirt blowing in the open windows stung her eyes. And, she'd reminded him at least twice, she had to get home as early as possible tonight because she had to count some weird bird at daybreak.

He figured he knew what was bothering her, and it was none of those. The attraction that had propelled them into a fast and short-lived affair was still there. That kiss in the playground was ample proof.

Miranda could say what she wanted about them being better off as old acquaintances, but he knew better. She would never have kissed him back if all she wanted was friendship. Hell, it was more like she'd have stomped on his foot and kneed him.

Nah, she liked him. Wanted him. The vibes she was giving off were only part of it. Like how she sat way over there, as if she couldn't keep her hands off him if she was closer. And those little things that bordered on flirting, like winding her hair around her finger, and the way she licked her lips.

Man, it was hard to imagine her as a mom. Even harder to think of her holding some guy's hands and gazing into his eyes as she said "I do." Her ring finger was as tan as the rest of her hand, and he wondered if her happily-ever-after with the kid's dad had turned into a disaster. Or maybe the guy skipped when she told him she was pregnant. She still used the Coulsen name.

"Are you sure we're going the right way?" Tension filled Miranda's voice as she looked one more time in vain for a map in the glove compartment.

"There's a road sign." Rik pointed toward a battered piece of tin on two rusty metal posts. "We're headed in the right direction."

"When we get there, you're going to look like you just stepped out of a shower and I'm going to look horrible." She frowned down at her linen slacks and shirt, her hand automatically going to her head to check out the condition of her hair. "If I'm ever stuck going any place with you again, I'm driving."

"There's a little restaurant on the edge of town where you can fix up while I have a cup of coffee. We're a little early. You can take all the time you need."

"I wouldn't need to stop in some greasy spoon and do my hair if you hadn't driven this stupid truck."

Rik's grip on the steering wheel tightened. "I would have been an idiot to use the car. It's meant for freeways and pavement, not dirt roads and potholes, like we're going to hit pretty soon."

"If you weren't so determined to be king of the world, you'd have let me drive. Oh, I forgot. You're the big man who gets to decide everything, like my car isn't good enough for you to ride in,"

Rik slammed on the brakes; the truck shuddered to a stop in the middle of the road.

"Enough already." He turned to face Miranda, not surprised to see her squish even tighter against the door. "I know you're hot, being a sensitive Midwesterner and all, but suck it up. And please don't tell me your damned government car is cold enough to keep meat. I checked it out when you got that flat tire, remember, and that piece of junk should have been retired before you were out of diapers."

"Look..."

"I'm not done yet." He held up a finger to silence her. "You've had a bug up your butt all day, and I'm tired of it."

"Excuse me?" Miranda's hands curled into fists. "Of all the pig-headed, egotistical cowboys in the West, I get stuck with you. In this bucket of bolts, which is barely big enough for you and your ego, let alone me."

"Randi, calm down."

"Do not call me Randi!"

She yanked on the door handle and half-fell out of the truck on her way out. Steadying herself, she hoisted her purse over her shoulder and began walking toward the town of Denton.

"Miranda, get back in the truck." She ignored Rik's plea and kept on walking, wishing she'd worn something other than espadrilles. She heard the low rumble as he shifted the truck into gear, but never slowed, her eyes focused straight ahead.

"You can't walk all the way to Denton," he shouted out the window at her. "It's at least 10 miles."

She ignored him and kept on walking.

"Be reasonable," Rik yelled.

Miranda focused on the road beneath her feet, taking one even step after another, moving steadily forward despite Rik's shout of "Fine then if that's what you want."

He coasted beside her for a few minutes before gunning the truck and taking off. Miranda's eyes filled with tears, but she willed herself not to let them fall. Let the SOB go to Denton without her. She'd get there under her own steam or die trying.

Ahead of her, Rik braked and jerked the steering wheel hard so the truck blocked the road. He jumped out and leaned against the battered fender, arms crossed.

She was almost past the truck when she sensed him moving toward her. She broke into a run, again silently cursing her choice in shoes, but he was too long-legged and fast for her to get away. He reached down and scooped her up, carrying her kicking and protesting to the truck.

"Let me down," she seethed, fighting his iron clasp. "I can't believe this is how you treat a woman."

He stopped so quickly she unconsciously stilled as well. He set her down gently and said, "Only the ones I care about," before kissing her.

She tensed, her hands flat against his chest. His lips were warm against her closed mouth, his arms firm around her body. The tension eased as he slipped the tip of his tongue between her lips and the palm of his hand against the back of her neck, coaxing her. Enticing her.

The tension faded, replaced by a longing that rocked her. The sizzle slid from their interlocked lips clear down to her toes, filling her, reminding her of what she missed by celibacy. She couldn't let him keep kissing her.

She couldn't bear not kissing him.

Her arms wound around his neck and she buried her fingers in his thick hair. Lost in the pleasure Rik offered, she forgot they were in the middle of a two-lane, blacktop road in the middle of nowhere. Forgot she was determined not to fall under his spell again, that she wanted to hate him. When he finally eased away, she nearly collapsed, her legs rubbery, her heart pounding and her whole being on fire.

Rik picked her up in a gentle clasp, and carried her back to the truck. Climbing in on the driver's side, he dropped the gearshift into drive and pressed down on the gas, as if the incredible thing that had just happened between hadn't.

Miranda found the refuge of the seat's edge, huddling against the passenger's door. Her body still tingling, she fought the pent-up desires demanding release now, immediately, without further delay. She was amazed and appalled by how quickly that need had come upon her, and furious with herself for having kissed him back. Until she'd seen Rick again, she been so sure she had him out of her system. Absolutely certain that the worries and hardships of the years since Brittini's birth had supplanted any leftover emotion. But she'd been wrong. Oh, man, had she been wrong.

They traveled in silence for the few miles to the small diner. Rik pulled into the graveled lot and parked by the front door.

"I'm getting coffee." He handed Miranda her purse. "The ladies' room is right inside, on the left."

Dropping onto a stool at the counter, he realized the separation as much as he needed the coffee. Kissing Miranda had been the farthest thing from his mind when he stepped out of the truck. He'd been more inclined to throttle her. He'd wanted to get her into the truck before she got heat stroke or broke an ankle on those silly shoes. When she challenged him, those brown eyes blazing, she had been simply irresistible. The years had slipped away and she'd been his Randi once more.

He'd wanted to please her again, as he had during those few precious weeks ten summers ago. He wanted to devour her, to possess her, to claim her as his own.

That scared the hell out of him. He wasn't a callow college kid, torn between angering his father and yearning for his first love. Now he was a man who understood responsibility. He finally realized what his dad had tried to tell him, that the philosophy of "if it feels good, do it" was failure in the making.

Trouble was, when he was around Miranda, that's all he could think of, how good doing it would feel.

"Refill, hon?" The question came from a plump, cheerful waitress standing beside him, coffee pot in hand. He looked down at his cup. It was empty, although he didn't remembering drinking. Man, he had it bad.

****

In the cramped restroom, Miranda yanked a brush through her obstinate hair, welcoming the sting as the bristles pulled through the knots. Dropping the brush back into her tote bag, she stared at herself in the mirror. She looked the same. That was odd, because on the inside, she was alive. Electrified. Giddy, to use her mother's word.

Miranda dropped down on the lidded toilet seat and buried her face in her shaky hands. If it wasn't for that damned meeting she'd spend the afternoon locked in here, trying to make sense of the dreadful truth: Despite all the heartache he'd brought her, she was still in love with Rik Hallowell–and she wanted nothing more than to go out there, grab him and drag him to the little motel across the street.

"Bad case of lust. That's all it is." She spoke the words out loud, as if hearing them would change how she felt. It didn't help. She still wanted Rik's body in a most desperate way. But there was a whole more to this craziness of hers. She liked his sense of humor and admired the way he treated people. She especially appreciated his relationship with Rosie, and the affection between them.

A tap on the door startled her.

"You okay in there? We need to get back on the road." Rik.

Taking a deep breath to steady herself, Miranda squared her shoulders and marched out.

"Hope I didn't take too long."

"Nah. It's fine. We do need to get going, though."

The few miles to their destination went by in silence. A barbecue was in full swing when they walked onto the grounds of the Moose lodge that had been rented for tonight's meeting. Small towns loved parties, Miranda had learned, but this cookout served a practical purpose too. Ranchers came for up to a hundred miles for a hearing, and few small-town restaurants could accommodate such a crowd.

When Rik recognized some friends, Miranda hung back, pleading the need for lemonade. She was on the job. Mingling with the ranchers and their wives, she made small talk as she got in line for ribs and potato salad. There would be time enough for serious talk when the meal was over.

"Don't say a word. I'm hungry." Rik came to sit beside her with his own plate heaped with barbecued ribs, baked beans and homemade bread.

Seating was snug, so his thigh was tight against hers. His hand occasionally rubbed against hers accidentally as he fumbled for the napkin on his lap. When he turned to greet a friend, his wide shoulder slid against her breast.

Once again, her body reacted in ways she hadn't expected. Heat rose in her lower body as his fingers slid across hers, at the richness of his laugh, the emptiness she felt when he rose and headed back to refresh their drinks.

"Your fella's a cutie," said the sun-worn woman in her seventies sitting on the other side of the picnic table.

"He's not my boyfriend. We rode together, that's all."

The woman grinned. "Go on and tell me another. I saw the way he looked at you, like he could eat you right up. If I were you, I'd grab him. He looks like a keeper to me."

Those words were a cold splash of reality. *The kind of fella a girl can depend on.* She'd thought so, too, until she learned Rik and commitment were leagues apart. His family's land mattered more than people or relationships.

Smiling goodbye, she went in search of him. She found Rik with a group of men, swapping jokes. She waved, and he joined her, a decidedly non-professional smile on his face.

"It's past time to start," she said, holding up her watch. "We set the meeting for seven, so you'd better get everyone inside."

Rik glanced at his own wrist. "It's only two minutes after, and eventually, they'll all wander in. Everyone's having fun, so what's your hurry?"

"I've got get an early start in the morning, and it's a long way home. We could be here a while if we get a lot of questions."

He shrugged and turned without speaking. She watched as he rounded people up and headed them toward the entrance to the building. Grabbing her briefcase from the truck, she made sure she was behind the podium before he came in himself. It was time to get this meeting, and her own unleashed feelings, back on track.

Her eyes narrowed when Rik stopped to speak to an attractive woman about her own age. Miranda was too far away to hear what he said, but they both laughed. She looked away when the woman reached up and rubbed his upper arm, as if she was trying to brand him.

A sick feeling welled up inside Miranda. An hour earlier, she'd been fantasizing about Rik and a motel room; that woman was probably imagining the same thing now.

Leaning toward the microphone, she said, "Good evening, everyone. If you'll all find a seat, we'll get started."

Rik took his time getting to the podium. When he finally arrived, Miranda stood back and waited as he gave a few preliminary remarks. He did a good job of summing up the situation of private grazing on public lands, and made her sound more important than she was with his introduction. As she replaced him at the mike, she reminded the audience their remarks would be forwarded to Congress and began accepting statements and questions.

Forcing herself to ignore the man sitting behind her, she made copious notes as the ranchers spoke. It was only after Rik began the wrap-up remarks that her mind wandered back to that kiss out on the highway. She should have ignored him and kept on walking. She should have slapped his face and told him never to try that again.

A sudden silence, and she realized Rik was done. Plastering on a smile, she said, "Thank you all for coming tonight, and be assured your voices will be heard in Washington. If you'd like to add written comments, feel free to pick up one of my cards from the table and send me a letter."

Back on the road to Armont, Miranda stared out the side window into the night sky. They were deep into the miles of empty when Rik said, "Those ranchers had a lot to say tonight, didn't they?"

"Uh-huh." She kept her gaze out the window to where the sunset painted pink and orange against the sky.

"I liked that old guy's suggestion that senior citizens get a discount, didn't you?"

"Makes sense to me," she said.

"And that lady rancher who inquired about bonus land for heifers. That was a pretty good idea, too, huh?"

"Yep. Really persuasive."

"Want to tell me what you're really thinking about? No one said a word about heifers."

"Whatever." Miranda closed her eyes, effectively ending his attempt at conversation. The sound of tires gave way to music when Rik snapped on the radio. Of course, it had to be a love-gone-wrong call-in show, and the mix of sad ballads of love betrayed, and visitors' stories of their own heartaches did nothing to improve her mood.

Maybe she'd make her own life into a country song, she decided, her mind drifting back to the first time she'd seen Rik. He'd been tall, lean, and the ultimate cowboy. His sexy eyes and western drawl had proved her downfall, but she wasn't a dewy-eyed teenager anymore.

Love at first sight was a joke. Happily-ever-after was a myth. She had to remember she wasn't Rik's girl anymore, she was Brittani's mom.

"Hey, our song." Rik turned up the radio, and a soft ballad filled the air. Miranda eyes filled as Garth Brooks' voice filled the cab, transporting her back to a time when the world had been new and anything possible, even love that lasted beyond a lifespan on earth.

She reached out and switched off the radio, ignoring Rik's protest. She'd had enough of memories for the night. She remembered every detail of falling in love. Now she had to figure out how to fall out of it, and fast.

# Chapter Six

Standing under the fine shower spray, wincing as needles of water pelted his back, Rik felt like a sixteen-year-old again. He'd been half-wild, crazy in lust with a girl who wouldn't give him the time of day, and spent his time depressed and lovesick in his room. His dad's cure was to send Rik out to buck bales of hay in the widespread pastures. Sore muscles and resentment at his father had helped him forget the girl pretty quick.

He'd spent the entire day in the same kind of mind-numbing labor, determined to drive Miranda from his mind, but to no effect. The way she ran hot and cold around him still confused him. What was he supposed to think when one time she kissed him like she was desperate for him and the next moment acted as if he was some pervert stalking her?

He'd called Miranda to ask her out to dinner on Friday. She'd acted as if he'd invited her to her own hanging.

Shutting off the water, he stepped out of the tub and began toweling dry. He desperately needed a diversion, because he was done panting after Miranda like a kid. Maybe it was time to start dating some of those women Rosie had sicced on him. Maybe tonight's trip to the Cattleman's with Junie ought to be a real date.

An hour later, he was escorting Junie into the Cattleman's Club. Rik ordered a steak and a beer; Junie ordered a salad and a fruity drink made with gin. While he dug into his meal with gusto, she only picked at her food and filled the time with two more drinks.

"The place is pretty full tonight," Rik said as the waitress removed their plates.

"Because it's karaoke night." Janie smiled and looped her fingers into Rik's. She also leaned forward to allow him a good look at her admittedly nice cleavage.

"Uh-huh." Janie didn't seem as eager as the other competitors. While they were signing up and checking on music, she slid even closer to him and talked. And talked and talked.

The first folks had already taken the mike when she kissed him on the cheek, promised she'd be right back and went to add her name to the performance sheet. He signaled the server for another drink and settled back to listen. The first singers were good; a number of them sounded like they ought to be on country radio.

As time went on, Rik watched in amusement as his inebriated friends took their turns at the mike. Every now and then, one of them would yell at him to get up and sing, too, but he stayed planted firmly in his chair. He'd switched to soft drinks because he was driving, and was way too sober to make a fool of himself.

Junie switched to tequila shooters after her first round qualifier, pouring them down like they were ice water. When her name was announced to come back up, she drained her glass and shouted, "I'm on my way."

Smooching Rik's lip, she made her unsteady way to the stage. She took the three small steps cautiously on her five-inch heels before settling on a stool by the screen.

Holding the microphone close, she said, "I'm dedicating this to that sexy guy over there," pointing a long red-tipped fingernail at Rik. "The one Lady Luck will be smiling on tonight."

Rik sank down in the booth, plastered a smile on his face and hoped booze improved her singing voice.

It didn't. Even worse, she had lousy taste in music.

"I love this song and I hope you do too," she shouted before launching an enthusiastic but out-of-tune song about riding on the sin wagon. Rik held up his hands in mock surrender when a couple of his buddies saluted him with their beer bottles.

"You got yourself a hot one," one of them shouted to him over the music as he passed on his way to the restrooms in the back. "We know what you'll be doing tonight."

*Dumping her at her place and getting the hell out of there.*

"So what did you think, baby?" Junie was back, sliding into the booth beside him and clamping a red-nailed hand on his thigh. "One more round and somebody's going to get the money."

Rik wanted to hand the woman her purse and drag her out of the Cattleman's and get gone. Instead, he moved her hand, scooted away and said, "It's too stuffy in here to sit so close."

"We could go outside," Junie offered. The words were ordinary; her tone was suggestive.

"Let's just stay here. We'll lose the booth if we leave."

Junie dropped her lower lip into a pout and tipped her head toward him, a pose Rik suspected had worked more than once. It didn't affect him. He was immune to the charms of sexpots, thanks to a decade of bad experiences. All he wanted was go home and climb into bed. Alone. He was tired, his muscles still ached, and this whole evening had been a mistake.

When the top competitors were announced for the final round, Junie's name wasn't among them. Rik wasn't surprised but Junie seemed upset. She quickly accepted his suggestion that they leave before the finalists took the stage.

"If we slip out now, no one will notice," he said as he motioned for the waitress to settle their bill. Ten minutes later, he'd pulled up by her house. He was gentleman enough to open the car door for her and walk her to her front door. But when she smiled up at him and said, "Are you sure you don't want to come in for a bit?" he ignored the hint, the same way he ignored her leaning toward him for a goodnight kiss.

A rush of relief flooded through him when she went through her front door without protest. He'd thought spending an evening in the company of some woman that wasn't Miranda would be a good thing. It had been a disaster.

During the few miles that took him back to the ranch, he thought about heading to her cabin to see if Miranda was still up. They hadn't talked about the meeting in Denton and he wanted her opinion about how things went before they did the next one.

"Yeah, right," he muttered as he drove past the turnoff that would have taken him there. He had to face the truth: he wanted a few moments with her as an antidote to having spent the evening with Junie.

The next morning, in the cold light of day, he vowed never to repeat the lapse in judgment that had led to his embarrassment. No more dates with strangers. Then again, Miranda had been a stranger when they met on that train ten years ago. He'd noticed her as soon as she climbed onto the train, couldn't believe it when she sat across from him. Her looks attracted him first, but the bubbly person inside was what he fell for. All he did was offer to help her with her tote, and she was chatting away like she was his best friend.

"Rik! Your breakfast is getting cold!" Rosie's shout up the stairs jolted him back to the present and the work that still waited to be done. Work Ron hadn't bothered with. Once again, this damned ranch came first, and his own problems second.

"Rik, I'm throwing your food outside to the dogs." Rosie's warning voice came up the stairs again.

"I'm on my way." He pulled on his scuffed boots and headed downstairs. Nothing could be gained by looking back. He'd worked sixteen-hour days getting to the top at Domino, and if he had to, he'd do the same thing to bring the Hallowell ranch back to its old glory. A few more weeks, and the physical work would be done. A month or two more of plowing through financials and trying to make sense of Ron's half-assed records, and he'd be able turn it over to a manager.

Then he'd be back at Domino. Back in the city. Someplace where memories never became dreams in the middle of the night.

A plate of eggs, bacon and biscuits was at his seat when Rik dropped into his chair at the table. Rosie waited until he'd eaten a few bites and gulped down some coffee before sitting down across from him.

"How was your date?"

"It wasn't a date. Miranda and I had another ranchers' meeting."

"That was three days ago." Rosie wasn't going to let him off the hook that easily. "I'm talking about last night. I heard you took the Delacroix girl to the Cattleman's Club, and she was all goo-goo eyed over you."

"Goo-goo eyed. Can you define that precisely?"

"Don't change the subject." Rosie's voice was determined. "I thought she wasn't your type."

"She's not." Rik shuddered at the memory of Junie's voice butchering what used to be an okay song. "Once was enough."

"Still, it was a date." Rosie worried the subject like a dog with a bone. "That's good. If you don't date, people are going to think that there's something wrong with you."

"You mean they'll think I'm gay?" He wanted to laugh, but he knew better.

"No, they'll think you're scared of settling down. They'll think you don't care whether or not there's a next generation of Hallowells on this ranch, after 100 years."

"Ron's got a wife," Rik pointed out.

"Her?" Rosie snorted. "She'd never have a baby. She couldn't stand to have that perfect body imperfect even for a little while." She stood and nodded her head, as if she'd settled something.

"I'm going to town. Eat your breakfast. Have more coffee."

As soon as his mouth was full, she added, "By the way, Miranda just pulled up outside. You better go tell her hello." She grabbed her purse and was gone, leaving him alone to face Miranda and whatever mood she might be in.

Rik abandoned his breakfast for the porch.

"Morning," he said, settling into one of the cedar chairs on the wide porch. "You're out early. Have a seat."

"I can't stay." Her voice was professionally cordial, her manner wary. "I need your signature on this consent form to allow me to go onto your land. There seems to be a pattern of animals crossing through. I suspect you have a natural water source."

"Have a seat," Rik repeated. "I need to read these papers before I sign them."

"I prefer to stand."

"Suit yourself." Rik shrugged. "I'll be right back. I've got a cup of coffee going cold in the house. Should I bring you some?"

"Don't bother." She spoke too late. Rik was already through the door, and she suspected he hadn't heard her. Lovely. If he brought coffee, would she be rude to refuse it? Frank would think so, and with her luck, he'd heard that she insulted the mighty Rik Hallowell. If she accepted it, Rik might think the consent form was simply an excuse to see him again.

She would have been smart to come in the afternoon. Miranda had always liked the way he looked when he first woke up, like a little kid, with his hair tousled and his face soft from sleep. She hadn't been prepared to see him like that. Since that moment on the road with the calf, old memories insisted on popping up at the most unexpected times, ones she thought he'd buried. Only the day before, when a baby wildcat ran in front of the truck, she'd suddenly remembered the half-grown stray cat he'd adopted during their time together.

"Here." Rik returned with two mugs. "Lots of cream, little bit of sugar."

"I use sweetener now." She accepted the coffee, careful not to let her fingers touch his.

"You don't need to." Rik looked her up and down, his study slow and thorough. "You look fine. But I suppose I can't really know for sure until I see you naked, can I?"

He grinned wickedly, his eyebrows rising in a fake leer, and Miranda couldn't decide whether to laugh or be mad. He'd always said outrageous things, and apparently time hadn't changed that either.

"Just read the papers, Rik."

She sipped as he scanned the form, staring out over the ranch. She about choked when he said, "I spent last night fantasizing about you."

"Oh, really?" The sarcasm in her voice was nothing compared to the withering look she directed his way. "Was that before you took June Delacroix out and got her drunk, or after you got her home? Or perhaps it was during whatever goodnight activity the two of you enjoyed?"

"So you're keeping up with what I do in my free time, are you? That's interesting."

"It's a small town and new travels fast." No way was she going to tell him about Junie's challenge earlier in the week, or what she'd heard over breakfast at the diner this morning about Junie sticking to Rik like Teflon to a skillet. She might be new in town, but she'd already learned Junie was husband-hunting with a passion.

Or so people said, she reminded herself. Small town folks were prone to gossip.

"Jealous, are you?" Rik drawled. "If it makes you feel better, I didn't kiss her goodnight."

"Like I care who you do or do not kiss."

Rik set down his mug, walked over and cradled her chin, gently bringing her eyes to meet with his.

"I saw her to her door, like the gentleman my mama expects me to be, but I definitely did not do this." He bent down and captured Miranda's lips in a kiss that was anything but cursory. She resisted until his hand moved to her cheek, gently caressing, and his tongue slipped into her mouth. The familiar ache began low in her belly as he pulled her close, and she was lost. Completely and totally lost. It felt so right to have his mouth on hers, his body against her, his touch both sensuous and demanding.

Rik's hand slid under her work shirt, his fingers splaying across her narrow back. She felt the hard ridge of his erection against her belly as his mouth moved from her swollen lips to the soft column of her neck. Sense warred with sensation until she finally pushed him away, sagging against the porch post in emotional and physical turmoil.

Rik leaned against the post opposite her and said quietly, "When we first met, we were both kids and didn't know how to handle ourselves, let alone how to treat each other. It's been nearly eleven years. We're two adults. We should be able to be honest with each other.

"Tell me you're not attracted to me and I'll tell you you're a liar. Tell me it's nothing more than a woman needing a man, and vice versa, and I'll call you a liar again. I've never been able to have a serious relationship with another woman, and obviously, you've been the same way, or you'd have a ring on your left hand. I think we need to own up to what's happening here and let things take their course."

Miranda was furious with herself for letting him get through her defenses, furious with him for his assumption that he could kiss any time he wanted.

"Some things never change," she said hotly. "All there's ever been between us, then or now, is lust. Pure and simple. Yeah, we were young and I was stupid." She started to shake, and hoped it didn't show in her voice. "I'd never met a real, live cowboy before, and I must have been an easy pick-up. We had both opportunity and raging hormones, and for three weeks, you indulged yourself.

"A lot of water has passed under the bridge since then. Leave things alone, Rik. Friendship I might manage, but nothing more. Do you understand that? I won't risk my heart again. I've got too much at stake now."

She tore down the steps and raced to her vehicle, roaring away from Rik and the ranch in a whirl of dust, the permission form forgotten. He stood on the porch, staring after her, totally perplexed. All he'd done was kiss her. He'd wanted to do a whole lot more, like carry her upstairs, lay her across his bed and spend all day making love to her the way he wanted to and she deserved.

He sighed and tossed his cooling coffee in a wide arch toward the lawn. He could figure out most women, but when it came to Miranda, he was clueless. He supposed he always had been.

Damn, but she'd been something back then. Nineteen years old, soaking in every new sight and experience with breathless excitement. At what he'd thought was the vast age of almost twenty-one, he'd considered himself sophisticated and experienced. It was his suggestion that they run off together, defy the expectations their families had and make their own way in the world.

Looking back, he could see they'd been too immature to make that kind of commitment. She'd been a college student on a big adventure, a trip to a friend's wedding in California before she started hitting the books in Michigan again. He'd been trying to find out where he fit in the scheme of things, chafing against his father's rules and eager to find himself. Maybe she remembered it differently, but Miranda was the one who'd suggested he come back here and settle things with his father instead of returning to Michigan with her.

"Get over it, man." Rik took the empty cups to the kitchen before heading for the truck. He had a morning of errands ahead of him, from picking up calf vaccine at the farm supply store to stopping by the bank to go over the farm accounts. He'd wasted enough time already. He had a ranch to run, a chunk of land that was a jealous mistress demanding his time, loyalty and money. To hell with the past; he had the future to worry about now.

## Chapter Seven

"I...cannot...believe...this."

Frustrated, Miranda punctuated every word with a kick to her broken-down sedan's bumper, wondering what the hell she was supposed to do now. This hunk of junk had given a big, tinny gasp and died out here where she was more likely to see an elephant than a tow truck. The battery on her cell phone was dead, which probably didn't matter anyway, since service out here was iffy at best.

Naturally, no one knew where she was. Working alone, she set her own schedule. Although a slice of daylight illuminated the long stretch of pasture, it was getting dark far faster than she liked. Another few minutes, and she'd be deep in the kind of twilight she connected with vampires and marauding coyotes.

Her brain began to retrieve a half-remembered and formerly useless piece of trivia about how long it took to die of dehydration. Longer than starvation, she was sure. She'd read once about someone who survived by straining urine and drinking it, but she had no intention of doing that. She'd die first, thank you very much.

A tip from a long-ago driver's ed class came to mind. She fished around in the back seat until found a white t-shirt. She yanked it down over the bent antenna. If someone did happen by, maybe they'd recognize it as a distress symbol.

"Not with my luck," she said aloud. She needed to hear a voice, even if it was her own. "They'll think I'm drying my laundry."

She climbed into the car, rolled up the windows and locked the doors. Her growling stomach reminded her she'd been too upset over the scene with Rik to eat lunch. A search for anything edible resulted in a half-pack of gum from the bottom of her purse and a package of outdated crackers in the glove compartment. Her tiny stash started to look more and more tempting as full dark settled around her, but she wasn't sure it was wise to eat crackers without something to wash them down.

She sighed and settled against the seat. At least she wasn't totally in the dark. The tiny book light she'd bought to use on the airplane coming out here still had some battery power. If she nursed it, she might make it till morning without going nuts.

In the daylight hours, someone was bound to come along. This wasn't much of a road, but it was a road. A sudden, horrible thought struck her. She sat upright and began to worry anew.

What if by some horrid coincidence it was Frank? He'd understand that she couldn't have stopped herself from having car trouble, but he'd probably blab that she had been totally unprepared for an emergency. Then she'd be in the field office typing reports, and perfect Derek would be here. He'd probably come prepared with a case of bottled water, a stash of irradiated meals and a signaling device.

Miranda stared out the window, her unease growing. She didn't like this, not one bit; she had no choice but to stay put. Sighing, she settled back in the seat again, trying to envision the distance from here to Armont. And wondering whether the boredom or a coyote would kill her first.

She was sound asleep when a rap sounded on her window. Instantly awake, she jumped, banging her head on the window glass. A large, dark shape hulked outside the door; it was all she could do to keep from screaming.

"Miranda, are you okay?" The voice, muffled by the glass, was all too familiar.

"Yes," she said, opening the door and stepping out without meeting Rik's eyes. If he said even one word about her getting stuck out here, she was getting back in.

"Pop the hood," he said, moving around front to peer at the engine. The high-beam emergency light he held cut a swath in the darkness. He fiddled with something before yelling, "Try it!" at her. She got back in and turned the key, but nothing happened. Even after ten minutes of jiggling this and wiggling that, her car was as dead as ever.

"Got me." Rik shrugged and wiped his greasy hands on his jeans. "But I know more about cows than cars, so I'm probably the last person you need right now."

"Thanks anyway," she said.

He gave up on his hands and leaned against the fender she'd been abusing earlier. "What are your plans?"

"I thought I'd sit here a while and see if it would start like magic."

"Tsk, tsk." Rik waggled a finger at her. "Sarcasm is not necessary, especially at..." he glanced at his watch... "just a little shy of midnight on a weeknight." He straightened and said, "Hop in with me. I'll take you to the ranch."

"You mean you'll take me home," she corrected.

"Nope." He started for the truck. "It's a couple of miles to my house and about fifteen to yours. If you want to go any further than the ranch, plan on walking. It's late, I've got to get an early start in the morning, and I'm not going to waste an hour getting you to your own bed before I get to mine. Nothing will be hurt but your feelings if you put up at my place again tonight."

Miranda's hesitation was short-lived. Beggars can't be choosers, as her dad always said.

"Talk about déjà vu," Miranda muttered to herself half an hour later as she slid into the same borrowed nightgown in the same room at the ranch. She'd taken a quick shower and brushed her hair with the small brush she carried in her purse, her exhaustion growing with each movement. Turning back the covers, she climbed into bed and this time she zonked out as soon as her head hit the pillow. Her last thought before she slid into darkness was that Frank was seriously going to get a piece of her mind this time.

Rosie's cheery knock on the door woke her early the next day, and she climbed back into her wrinkled clothes with a grimace of distaste. She could hardly wait to get home and change.

Rik was in the kitchen, drinking coffee, when she walked in.

"I called the tow truck for you," he announced without as much as a simple hello first. Although she knew it was petty, Miranda resented his abrupt manner. Not that she blamed him. She had been pretty snippy with him last night. "Do you think the mechanic can fix it this afternoon?" She poured her own coffee and seated herself at the table.

Rik laughed. "You'll be lucky if Fred gets it towed today. When you're the only mechanic in town, and the only tow truck, you're kept hopping."

"But I've got to get out in the field." Miranda was dismayed. How in the world could she get any work done if she had to walk everywhere?

Rik snapped his fingers, as if struck by a sudden thought. "That paper you left. That was so you could count flora and fauna here on the ranch, right?"

"Well, just fauna, yeah."

"Then ride with me."

"Excuse me?" Did Rik really think she could hop out of his truck and start counting whatever moved any place he chose?

"I've got to check on some cattle we moved up to the high ground," he explained, "and drive along the fence line and see if there are any more weak spots. My brother was more interested in boffing his wife than keeping up this place, and I'm still fixing things he let go."

"That might work," Miranda said slowly, her voice clouded with doubt.

"Why wouldn't it?"

Miranda could think of a million answers to Rik's question, from not trusting herself in such close proximity to worrying about what people would say.

"You haven't given me a reason yet." Rik stared across the table at her, his brown eyes intense. She could tell she wasn't going to wiggle out of this one. She reluctantly agreed, certain deep inside that she was on the verge of another disaster.

The morning went smoothly, far better than she'd feared. Rik dropped her off on his way to check the herd, and stopped by around noon to find her less than a half-mile from where he'd left her.

"Counting snails?" he teased.

"Actually, I haven't counted much of anything," she admitted. "I've spent the time since you've been gone mapping out the paths the critters take. They move from shade to water to food, you know, and don't much care who owns the land. Once I figure out their paths, I'll come around sundown and count species as they go move when it cools off." She grinned up at him. "Except for federal employees and dedicated ranchers, most living things stay where it's cool instead of out in the open at midday."

"I know a cool place," Rik suggested, reaching down and pulling her up from where she sat cross-legged on the ground. "How do you feel about air conditioning, beer, and burgers as big around as a dinner plate?"

"Hmmm." Miranda tapped her chin, pretending to think. "Either you're taking me to that new restaurant in Denver that's the new hot spot for the elite, or you're talking about the Cattleman's."

Rik laughed. "I'd prefer Denver myself, but we'd starve before we got there in this old truck. So you up for a burger?"

"Only if it's Dutch treat," she agreed. "Two people having lunch, nothing more."

"It could be more," he teased as they got into the truck. "Like their specialty dessert that involve whipped cream and cherries. We could get those last two things to go."

"As if."

He ducked as Miranda punched his shoulder, relieved that whatever bee she'd had in her bonnet had finally flown away. He still didn't what he'd done to tick her off. She'd been fine ... heck, way past fine ... until the end of that barbecue. Since then she'd been colder than Santa's nose at the North Pole. But now that she was thawing out, maybe he could turn the heat up a little.

He asked about her work, a question she answered in great detail with enthusiasm, not stopping until they arrived at the restaurant. She showed more passion talking about migration trails and mating habits of opossums than she did about human beings, he decided. He was still having trouble reconciling this Miranda with the Randi of so many years ago.

The hum of conversation permeating the restaurant stopped momentarily as they walked in. Rik watched a delicate blush stain Miranda's cheeks, and realized she was really was worried about the town gossips. He thought her concern was cute. He couldn't remember the last time he'd been with a woman who worried more about her reputation than spending his money.

He nodded at the men who openly stared at them. The few women in the place for lunch were more discreet, their glances sliding toward the two of them and quickly moving away. Rik still wasn't sure who gossiped the most, the men at the barbershop or the women at the beauty salon.

They were halfway through their cheeseburger when the door swung open and Junie sashayed in. Rik looked, of course; every man in the place did. Junie in a swinging skirt that barely covered her butt, a tee tied in a knot under her ample bosom and three-inch heels were a sight few red-blooded men could ignore.

He tensed as she made her way directly to the booth where he sat with Miranda.

"Hey, honey." Junie sat beside him and nudged him over. "I had a blast the other night. Both here and…well, you know."

She wrapped a hand around his arm and squeezed slightly, smiling up at him like they shared some big secret.

"My mama had to have those tests in Denver this week, and I couldn't let her go alone, even though it turned out she's fine. I'm so silly. I should have given you my cell number."

She grabbed a napkin and waved the waitress over. Borrowing the woman's pen, she jotted her number down and tucked the napkin into Rik's jeans pocket.

"Ready for more karaoke on Saturday?"

"I don't know when I'll have free time again." Rik chose his words carefully. He'd rather kiss a polecat than spend five minutes alone with Junie again, but this wasn't the place to tell her so.

"Just give me a call when you're free." She winked. "Or come by. Any time."

Before Rik could react, she leaned over and pressed her lips to his. He glanced at Miranda as Junie walked away, and realized she would never believe he had no interest in the woman.

Before he could even begin to explain that Junie was a big, fat liar, Miranda pushed her cheeseburger away. Her face was pale, her shoulders squared. He couldn't decide if she was angry, hurt or both. He knew better than to ask.

"I'm ready," she said, the words coming through tight lips.

"I'm not." Rik picked up his own sandwich. If he stalled, maybe she'd calm down enough that they could talk about this.

"Knock on the restroom door when you are." She was gone.

Miranda saw no one, focused on nothing but the hand-painted sign that said "Heifers" as she sought the refuge of the ladies lounge. Built in the club's former, classier days, the lounge had an anteroom with two chairs and a huge potted plant. She planned to stay planted on one of those chairs until she could make her escape.

The door opened before she could sit down and Junie strolled in. Miranda braced herself for a verbal barrage, or even a thrown punch, but Junie was calm. She checked her make-up in the mirror before turning to Miranda and looking her up and down.

"Nice outfit," she said, sarcasm underscoring her words. "Nothing turns a man on more than khaki shorts and hiking boots."

Miranda was in no mood to beat around the bush. "You're welcome to the man. I don't want him."

Junie wiped a smudge of red lipstick from the corner of her mouth and smiled. It was a deliberate attempt to remind her of that kiss a few minutes ago, Miranda realized. Junie's deep inhalation and gradual exhalation was another not-so-subtle reminder of what she had and Miranda didn't.

"All you are is a change of pasture," Junie said. "If you think you're more to him than summer fun, forget it. He's not the kind of man to go without a woman for long, and with me in Denver, he's had to find some sort of substitute. I suppose you were a change of pace, brains instead of beauty."

She stretched lazily and added, "Thanks for scratching his itch. I hope you understand when he quits calling. My poor darling has a low threshold of boredom."

Junie fluffed her hair and sauntered out, leaving Miranda with both her stomach and her fists in knots.

"Low threshold of boredom," she parroted. "Change of pace." She squared her shoulders and began to pace.

She stalked the small anteroom, getting angrier as Junie's insulting words rolled around in her mind. She wasn't supposed to look sexy. She was supposed to look competent. That didn't mean she couldn't give Rik as good a time as Junie and her stripper boobs.

She yanked open the door and walked back toward the booth, where Junie was now occupying her seat. What a cozy tete-a-tete, she decided bitterly, with Junie leaning forward to give Rik a good look down her cleavage, and him smiling like a polecat.

Everyone at the Cattleman's saw them, which meant that everyone in Armont would know Junie had come into the place and basically run her out. If she let that happen, that was.

Putting as much sway in her walk as she could in high-top boots, she made her way back to Rik. She slid in beside him, forcing herself to smile at Junie.

"Do they talk walk-ins at the beauty shop?" she asked in her best honeyed tones.

Junie nodded, her long blond curls bobbing. Miranda leaned forward.

"You might want to go in for an emergency appointment. I think I see some gray in those dark roots of yours."

She heard Rik stifle a laugh. Emboldened by his reaction, and Junie's shocked face, she added, "And it might be time to wax those little hairs off your lip again."

This time, Junie gasped aloud. A surge of triumph welled in Miranda who, propelled by that triumph, turned to Rik and kissed him. Really kissed him, not a peck on the lips, or a brush across his mouth, but the way a woman kissed a man she cared about.

When she opened her eyes, Junie was gone. Rik pulled back and stared at her, his eyes wide. She knew he expected an explanation, but she was damned if he was getting one. Maybe Junie was right and he was trying to use her for a summer fling. But like her grandmother always preached, what was good for the goose was good for the gander.

"Let's get out of here," she said, sliding out of the booth and grabbing her purse.

"Sure." Rik quickly followed, dropping money on the table to cover the bill. When she took his hand as they walked out, Miranda knew the news would be back to Junie by nightfall.

"What was that all about?" he asked as they drove out of Armont.

"Do you think I'm sexy?"

He stared at her, wondering if it was a trick question.

"I'm not in the habit of kissing women who turn me off."

"Am I as sexy as she is?"

Okay, now he knew where she was coming from. He'd seen Junie go into the ladies room and come back out, but she hadn't been in there long. Apparently, her stay had been enough to piss Miranda off.

"Hey, don't compare yourself to Junie. All she has is a hot body."

"Yeah, it's pretty obvious she doesn't have kids."

Ah, there it was, the source of Miranda's insecurity. Rik wanted to reassure her. He wanted to tell her she was beautiful, but better than that, she was the combination of smart, sweet and sassy that attracted men for more than a night.

"What do you cowpokes do for fun?" Miranda asked suddenly, while he was still framing an answer.

"Besides poke cows?" he asked. "There's bingo at the church basement tomorrow night, a dance by the Jaycees Saturday at the school, and on Sunday, the annual carry-in dinner at the church. That's about all."

"Will Junie be at the dance?"

"Junie will be wherever there are men," Rik said drily. "Young men, old men, married men, single ones. Her standards are pretty broad."

"You're not asking her to go?" she shot him a sidelong glance.

"Lord no." He suppressed a shudder at the thought. The last place he wanted to be with Junie Delacroix was where there was close dancing.

"So how about going with me?"

His hesitation was momentarily, only long enough for him to frame and reject the possibility that this might be another trick question. He didn't know why she'd changed her mind, or what she expected from him, but he didn't care. Dim lights, dance music, his arms around Miranda with their bodies in close contact…whatever price he might have to pay, it would definitely be worth it.

## Chapter Eight

The sun-dappled room in which Miranda awoke had become familiar. The scent filling the air, however, was different from the usual aroma of bacon and eggs. One deep breath, and she realized the scent was sweet and tempting. She discovered a plate of hotcakes already waiting for her when she walked into the kitchen, with a pitcher of Rosie's homemade apple-cinnamon syrup warm in a pitcher beside them.

"I'm going to get fat if I keep eating like this," Miranda sighed as she picked up a fork. She'd been at the ranch for four days, waiting on her own set of wheels, and it was like staying in a wonderful B&B.

"You spend too many hours walking through the land around here to put on an ounce," Rosie replied. She slid a plate of spicy sausage patties toward Miranda. "Better get some of these before Rik shows up. If he gets to the table first, it's slim pickings for the rest of us."

"He's always been like that," Miranda spoke before she thought. At Rosie's sudden, narrowed-eyed stare, she added, "At least it seems that way. You can't believe how much he eats when we go somewhere."

"Seem likes you two have been going somewhere a lot lately."

Rosie's back was to the table as she whipped up another batch of pancake batter. Rosie's words were neutral, casual. Her face always told her emotions, though, and Miranda wished she knew whether Rosie was continuing the conversation or prying for information.

"He's doing me a favor," she said. "I don't want to get hit on while I'm here, and with Rik as my chaperone, other guys stay away."

She was definitely not going to tell Rosie about Junie. That would be like taking out an ad in the local paper.

"Oh." One syllable, yet that single word spoke volumes. Now Miranda was certain Rosie was fishing for details. Of course, the housekeeper might do the same thing when she saw Junie, too.

The Saturday night dance had turned out to be different, and more fun, than Miranda had anticipated. Surprised by how many people she knew at the event, Miranda fallen into conversation without her usual self-consciousness. Having Rik by her side helped. Normally, she was ill at ease in unfamiliar situations, unless the action took place in the great outdoors or within the strict confines of her parents' social circle.

"I sure hope it doesn't rain today." Miranda decided to change topics before Rosie finished cooking and settled down to chat.

"The weatherman says cloudy but no rain." Rik slid into a chair across from her, snagging two sausage patties. He forked a couple of pancakes onto his plate, loading them with butter and syrup.

"Are you going into town today?" Rosie poured his coffee as she spoke. "I need a few things from the store."

"Hadn't planned to. I can if you want."

"No, I'll go," Rosie said absently, as if her mind was far away. "I suppose you and Miranda will be busy today."

"I will be." Miranda got up and poured herself another cup of coffee. "I've got a ton of paperwork that I've been putting off."

Rik gulped down the last of his coffee and stood. "I've got a couple of guys coming to help round up the calves for branding." He glanced at the calendar hanging on the wall above Miranda's head as he settled his battered Stetson on his head.

"By the way, they're having line dance lessons at the senior center tonight. I'm thinking of brushing up my skills, in case you'd like to come with me."

Miranda frowned. "Don't you think we're a little young?"

Rik laughed. "The seniors make money off the rest of us to keep the center running. Two songs and they're begging off because of their arthritis."

"Oh, you definitely need to go," Rosie said, her eyes lighting up. "You can wear jeans and boots if you've got them, Miranda. Nothing fancy–"

"I'll be back by six," Rik interrupted. He sounded as if his patience with girl talk was wearing thin. "Maybe you'd like to have dinner at the Cattleman's before the dance."

"That's right, make an evening of it." Rosie's smile grew wider. "You kids work too hard. A little fun will be good for you both." After a slight pause she added, "Junie may be there, too. I heard at the beauty shop that she's sweet on you."

"We'll leave about six," Rik said directly to Miranda. He wore a frown between his eyes, and gave off an air of definite displeasure.

Miranda stayed quiet and sipped her coffee as Rosie handed Rik a bulging thermal lunch bag. She wasn't surprised when Rosie sat down for a chat as soon as the door slammed behind him.

"I worry about that boy," Rosie said. She picked up a salt shaker and began twirling it in her hands. "His father wanted him to take over this place and raise another generation of Hallowells. He's working himself to death trying to get it back in shape and take care of things back at his job. Most nights, he eats dinner at his computer and sometimes he'll be working in the study when I arrive in the morning."

Miranda realized what a great opportunity this was to find out what happened between Rik and his father. She'd seen how torn he was between Colorado and San Francisco first hand. It wasn't unusual for him to excuse himself during a cattleman's meeting so he could take a phone call, or for him to carry on a text conversation under the table.

Maybe she could discreetly pry…

"He could be on the computer chatting with a girlfriend."

Hazel snorted. "He'd have to get serious with a woman first. He's never brought a girl with him on a visit, and his mother says he's dating someone new every time she goes to see him. We both hoped he'd pick a girl back here, someone he had something in common with."

*Someone like Junie.* Junie's hurtful, smirking words came back to Miranda, and her challenge that Rik's only interest in Miranda was a temporary affair and casual sex. She glanced down at her usual outfit of khaki shorts and camp shirt, and sighed.

"When you say 'into town', what do you mean?" she asked Rosie.

"Any place with a supermarket bigger than the little store in Armont," she said. "Did you want to tag along?"

Miranda nodded. "I can put off my work for a while. Would your supermarket be anywhere near a mall?"

"Sure would." Rosie stood up, a huge smile on her face. "There are a couple of new stores with real cute things. You can be the belle of the ball tonight."

Looking in the mirror nine hours later, Miranda decided relying on Rosie's judgment might have been a mistake. Her new dress, a rich blue that set off her blond hair and tanned skin, was shorter than she usually wore, and cut low enough to show off the vee of her cleavage. Rosie had dragged her to the cosmetics counter, and the woman staring back at her had wide, sexy eyes and rich, red lips.

"You sure it's not too much?" She turned uncertainly to Rosie.

"Just right." The older woman sighed. "You'll steal every heart there."

Miranda laughed. "Oh, I don't want that. I haven't the slightest idea what I'd do with the hearts of every man in Armont."

The sound of boots in the hallway outside had Rosie quickly stepping out of the guest room and shutting the door. Miranda could hear her scolding Rik for being late before the door swung open again.

"He's getting ready," Rosie announced. "Now you get on downstairs and practice walking in those heels. They're pretty low, but all you wear are those ugly hiking shoes. I'd hate for you to trip and break your ankle."

By the time Rik made his own appearance, Miranda had mastered the shoes and was seated in the living room, heart beating like a drum. She was as nervous as a teenager going to her first prom, and this wasn't a date at all. She was using Rik and this new look to show a certain little witch she wasn't the only attractive woman on earth. That was all.

Or so she told herself as Rik stared at her with open admiration. Her nerves started to tingle as he slowly looked her up and down before uttering one simple word.

"Wow."

She'd expected some sort of compliment, a smooth line he'd used a million times on other women. All he said, though, was that one word, a second time, still staring at her.

"Are you ready?" she asked.

Whoa. Her voice was huskier than usual, as if it too was reacting to Rik's obvious interest in her as a woman. She took a deep breath and asked the question again, sounding normal this time.

"Whenever you are." Rik covered the few steps between them and offered his arm.

Miranda walked carefully behind him, mindful of the dressy shoes she wore. She held his arm as they walked out of the house and to his car, wondering for the hundredth time if this was a good idea. This afternoon, while shopping with Rosie, all she could think of was showing up Junie. Alone with Rik, she remembered how, when he'd gotten close enough to kiss her, he had–and that she'd kissed him back. Tonight, she felt sexy and reckless, a dangerous mood to be in when Rik

Hallowell was only an arm's length away. She might be older now, with a firmer grip on her emotions, but he was still the only man who'd never made feel this way.

"This isn't for me, is it?" A statement from Rik, not a question.

"Of course it is."

"You're trying to show Junie up, aren't you?"

"Mostly," Miranda said honestly. "She said some mean things to me, which I don't intend to pass on. She also helped me remember that working in a man's world, I sometimes wonder if people realize I'm a woman."

"Trust me, there will be no question tonight." Rik took her hand, lacing his fingers with hers. "I love the way you look. So will every other man at the dance. If any of them give you even a second of grief, stare at you wrong or say something out of line, they'll answer to me."

His features were serious in the dimming light, too serious for her well-being.

"Will you beat them up?" she teased.

"Don't worry about what I'll do," Rik replied without smiling. "Rest assured no one will bother you twice."

Rik found a parking place around the corner from the senior center in downtown Armont. Miranda didn't pull away when he took her hand as they started down the sidewalk. When they reached a puddle of darkness between two light posts, he said, "Slap me later if you want, but I can't resist doing this."

In the microseconds before his lips touched hers, Miranda thought of ducking away. They were playing with fire and she knew it. But like a moth entranced by a flame, she tipped her face toward him and closed her eyes. His kiss teased rather than fulfilled, made her insides quiver and her toes curl. Too soon it was over and he led her inside, where it seemed like half the folks in Armont watched them walk in.

Cold brown eyes locked on hers as Junie stared, her mouth tight. Miranda leaned into Rik and kept her lips turned up in a smile. "You're the most beautiful woman here," Rik whispered, as he opened his wallet and paid the admission cost. Miranda grasped her tiny borrowed purse with both hands, struck by the sudden certainty that her boss was somewhere in the crowd, watching her disapprovingly.

"Frank's not here is he?" she asked, scanning the crowd as Rik led her toward the dance floor. His hand cradled the small of her back as they found a place in the learner's line.

Rik was amused. "If he is, so what? It's Saturday night. You're a single woman, I'm a single man. Did you sign a morals clause when you took this job that said you have to live like a hermit until you leave Colorado?"

Miranda relaxed against him. Put that way, it was silly to worry. She was so immersed in the twin responsibilities of work and motherhood that she'd nearly forgotten how to relax. It was time she refreshed her memory.

In the front of the room, the young instructor demonstrated the steps they were about to learn. Miranda watched intently, trying not to remember that she had two left feet. She discovered as the music started that she wasn't the only one who lacked natural rhythm. Around her, others were stumbling and laughing, and she soon joined in.

****

Beside her, Rik managed not to knock anyone over or step on any feet but his own. Dancing wasn't his thing. Miranda was, and if he had to make a fool of himself on a dance floor to keep in her good graces, it was a small enough price.

By the time they'd practiced four dances, the entire room was full. The noise of laughter and voices rivaled the music as friends found one another. After the instructor proclaimed the lesson a success, Rik led Miranda to the concession stand.

Hazel stood behind the counter, passing out popcorn and soft drinks, while Rosie perched on a stool by a money box.

"You dance real good without those clodhoppers on your feet," she said, offering Miranda a teasing smile. "You're going to be a popular partner tonight."

She winked when Rik frowned and shook his head. Miranda had the impression she would have said something more if another customer hadn't shown up, money in hand. Rik took advantage of the interruption to lead the way to a corner away from the crowd.

Friends of Rik's drifted over to talk, their conversations centering on people and events Miranda knew nothing about. She watched the band set up and sipped her cola, well aware that Junie watched from across the room.

"Want to try some of those steps?" Rik asked as the first song began. At Miranda's nod, he took her glass and set it on the table behind them.

The dance went better than she expected. Her confusions were small and easily fixed by Rik's hand pulling her back into place. At the end of the song, he pulled her against him in a hug of celebration, and she didn't resist. She was having fun.

As Rosie had predicted, other men asked her to dance. She gracefully turned them down, not because of Rik's earlier attitude but because her toes were beginning to hurt in her new shoes. She laughed until her sides ached when Rosie and Hazel decided to give it a try and ended up going the wrong way, mixing everyone up until it looked like a human traffic jam.

Because the evening started early, it ended early as well. It was a little before ten when Rik went after the car. Although Miranda hadn't mentioned her aching feet, she suspected he guessed by how long she'd sat at the end of the dance.

Miranda waited for him outside the building, slipping off her shoes and leaning against the center wall. She jumped, startled, at a brisk tap on her shoulder. She turned to find Junie glaring at her.

"You may think that dressing like that and acting like butter won't melt in your mouth is going to get you Rik, but remember what I said." The other woman's words were bitter, although her voice was soft. "You're nothing more than summer fun, so enjoy it while it lasts. He won't even remember your name at Christmas when he's sliding an engagement ring on my finger."

Miranda expected her to slink away as Rik pulled up. Instead, Junie walked to his car door, leaned down and said something. She laughed and she straightened up, waving her fingers as she walked to the other side of the street. Instead of walking on, she stopped and watched as Rik opened the door for Miranda.

A sudden impulse drove Miranda to pull Rik's face down to hers, wrap her arms around his neck and kiss him as passionately as she could in a public place. She meant it for Junie's sake, but within seconds, she was kissing Rik for her own. For the feel of him, the taste of him, the ache building inside her. The sound of a loud wolf whistle broke them apart, and she ducked into the car, suddenly and incredibly embarrassed.

"I cannot believe I did that." She buried her face in her hands. "Sometimes I do the stupidest things."

Rik pulled onto the shoulder of the road.

"Look at me." He turned her toward him. "We got caught kissing. Big deal. It happens all the time to people. We're adults, and it's no one's business but our own."

"I'm too old to make out in public." Miranda pulled away and stared out through the windshield. "I should have known better."

"Why?" Rik's voice carried all his frustration of the last few weeks. "Why is it so wrong if you kiss me? Why is it so wrong if it goes further than that? We're two consenting adults, aren't we?"

"If it was just us, it wouldn't matter," Miranda spit out. "But it's not."

Rik stared at her, perplexed. "Who else is there? Your daughter? I'm not asking you for anything permanent. All I want is for us to get to know each other again, to see if there's anything left of what we had before."

"You don't know what you're asking." Miranda's response was barely a whisper.

"Maybe not." Rik started the car. "But sometime, you're going to tell me why we're playing this game."

They rode in silence until the lights of the ranch came into view. Rik pulled up in front of the house to drop Miranda off. As she reached for the door handle, she said, "You know, I really did have a nice time tonight. It was more fun than I'd expected. I hope Rosie didn't push you into this."

Rik's face was lost in dark of the car's interior, but she could hear truth in his voice when he spoke.

"Look, I never do anything unless I want. I like doing things with you. When you decide to take a chance on opening up to a man again, I want it to be me. Someday, Miranda, you're going to tell me why you built this wall around your heart, and I'm going to figure out how to knock it down. Now you'd better go on in or I'm going to kiss you again."

Miranda opened the door and slid out, slipping off her shoes to walk barefoot across the grass. His words rang through her mind, and she realized he meant them.

She hadn't expected this…whatever…between them. It went beyond physical desire, although there was plenty of that. She could see herself spending her life with this man, helping him run this ranch, raising his children and sitting out in that transplanted garden, both of them silver-haired, watching their grandchildren playing hide-and-seek.

*You're a fool*, she told the woman in the mirror as she washed off the make-up and brushed her stiff hair. *Dreaming of something that can never be*. She snapped out the light and undressed in the dark, carefully laying her new dress over a chair and slipping into the cotton nightgown. Fred had promised she'd have her wheels back no later than Monday. She would be so grateful to be back at her own place, far away from the temptations that Rik presented.

She punched her pillow, squirmed down under the covers and willed herself to go to sleep. But she couldn't will away the ache of wanting Rik, of needing more from him than a kiss or two. It was well toward dawn before she finally slipped off into a slumber filled with remembrances of past passion and the ache of a body unfilled, memories of a wide bed in a small hotel room, and the heavenly haven of Rik's arms.

# Chapter Nine

Sunday morning, Rik woke to the mixed scents of coffee and burning toast. Pulling on jersey shorts and a tee, he headed for the kitchen. It was Rosie's day off, so he and Miranda were alone in the house.

He found Miranda standing over the kitchen sink, scraping at a singed piece of toast with a butter knife.

"You know, you could throw that out." He poured himself a cup of coffee.

"It's not that bad." She kept on scraping, her back to him.

"Suit yourself." He reached into the freezer, pulled out a package of frozen waffles and slid two into the toaster.

He expected Miranda to sit down at the table, but she headed for the garden instead. He snagged his waffles when they popped up, slapped them on a plate and poured maple syrup over them. He headed out to the wrought iron table where Miranda sat.

"Here. I'm done." She got up as soon as he neared, leaving her chair pushed back for him.

He watched her retreat to the house, confused and frustrated by the way she ran hot and cold. Sometimes it seemed as if they were back in the old days, laughing together and carrying on mock debates about movies or television shows until Rosie would tell them to knock it off. Alone together…that was a different story. Even a blind man could tell there was some sort of friction between Miranda and Junie, and sometimes he felt like a pawn in a battle he was only peripherally involved in.

Giving up that line of thought, he washed down the last of his waffle with a final swallow of coffee. He could sit here all day and try to figure out women, or could go inside to his office and get some work done.

Several hours later, he heard a rap on his study. Miranda stood in the doorway.

"Hi." He leaned back from the computer and stretched his cramped muscles. "I lost track of time. Do you want to go into town for lunch?"

"Actually, I'd like to talk. Mind if I sit down?"

"Not at all." He waited as she settled on the black leather loveseat. "So what do you want to talk about?"

"The situation we're in."

"Your one-upmanship of Junie or the chemistry between us you refuse to acknowledge?"

"Forget Junie, let's talk about us." Miranda willed her voice steady. "You told me once how much you admire straight-shooters, so I'm going to be honest. These last few weeks, you've made it obvious you'd like another summer fling." She took a deep breath and continued, her fingers interlaced on her lap.

"You were right when you said we're different people now. I'm far more cautious. Part of that has come from experience, and part is because I have responsibilities now. Do I want to make love with you? Yeah. Am I going to? Definitely not."

She expected some sort of protest. Rik said nothing. She forced herself to sit unblinking as he stared at her, a frown creasing between his eyes. She tensed when he moved his chair backward, her heart pounding as he stood and came to prop himself on the desk beside her.

"You're right," he said, his voice low and husky, "I think about sex with you all the time. At night when I'm trying to go to sleep. In the car when we're going to a cattleman's meeting and your perfume drifts over to me. I'll promise not to make any moves in the future, if you make me a promise, too."

"Which would be?"

"Don't kiss me again like you did last night, unless you mean it as an invitation."

His voice was soft, silky, like the caress of fingertips upon skin. The look in his eyes was a reminder that she'd been as intense a player in this cat and mouse game as him.

"I guess what we need is to stay as far away from each other as we can. I'll be out of here by nightfall."

She rose and hurried toward the door. Rik caught her before she could escape.

"No. We need to pretend we've just met and forget about the past. We both have something to lose if you walk out now. I'll be back to lonely days and nights, and your boss will be disappointed to learn you're isolating yourself again."

"That sounds a little like blackmail."

"God, no." Rik looked shocked. "We may never be lovers again, but do we have to treat each other like strangers? Do we have to pretend the past never happened?"

Shaken, Miranda pulled away and practically ran out of the house. She wished they *were* strangers. If only they'd met now and not ten years ago...

She didn't really mean that. If they'd never met, she wouldn't have Brittani. She'd never have the richness motherhood had brought to her life.

Her first priority had to be Brittani. Miranda had never lied to her; she had let her know that like all her friends, she had a father, but that there were circumstances that kept them apart. Brittani would never know that Miranda hadn't told Rik of her pregnancy, would never find out that she'd been the result of a summer affair.

Rik watched from the study window as Miranda wandered through the garden, lost in her musings. She reminded him of his mother, who used the garden as a retreat when homesickness got the best of her. Mom was eager to see her sons married and a new generation of Hallowells on this land. Then she could move back to Virginia and her roots, knowing the ranch would remain in the family as his father had wanted.

He suspected Miranda was homesick, too. For her daughter, if not for her home. He'd walked in on chats between

Rosie and her that changed as soon as he appeared. With Rosie, she talked about her daughter, her parents, and the ordinary events of her normal life. With him, she discussed the grazing laws and the economics of farming.

Sighing, he went back to the documents he'd downloaded. Domino Industries was in delicate negotiations in a take-over attempt, and he needed to e-mail his take on the problems that faced the company to the rest of the board before another blasted web conference tonight. He welcomed the work. By concentrating on it, he could block out a particularly vexing woman and the challenge she presented to his sanity.

****

Miranda drove up to her cabin the next afternoon, pleased to be on her own again. Rosie had taken her to the garage before noon, and she'd been able to start a new section of ranch land, far from the Hallowell ranch house. Frank Jarrell had flagged her down as she left Armont. To her surprise, he'd greeted her with a smile and been lavish in his praise of her work so far.

She quickly showered, thrilled to be using own body wash and lotions again, and pulled on slacks and a shirt. Her hair went into a braid and she added a minimum of makeup. Tonight was another of the public meetings that all seemed to be in the middle of nowhere.

She was on the phone with Brittani when Rik pulled up. She was still talking as she walked to the car, saying a quick goodbye as she got in.

"My daughter couldn't wait until tonight to call." Miranda tucked the phone in her tote bag fastened her seat belt. "My folks took her to her first professional baseball game, and she was so excited. My dad has been a Detroit Tigers fan all his life, and I guess it's rubbing off."

"I bet you wish you'd been with her."

Miranda laughed. "I hate baseball. It takes forever to play, and I don't understand the umpire's signals. I'm sure Brittani had a lot more fun without me."

After another question or two, Miranda realized they'd ventured onto dangerous ground. She deftly turned the conversation to the meeting ahead, leaving Rik no choice but to follow her lead. Once again they chatted about cattle prices and water rights, both of them aware of their promises the night before.

"The dress worked," Hazel said as she sat in the ranch house kitchen, stirring her usual two teaspoons of sugar and two tablespoons of cream into a cup of fresh coffee.

"So did some competition." Rosie giggled at the memory of Junie's eyes bugging out as she got her first look at the new Miranda.

"Sure did." Hazel sipped her drink and sighed. "I figured things would be moving faster than they are, though."

Rosie frowned. "Me, too."

The women sat in companionable silence, each lost in her own thoughts.

"I believe I'm coming down with a summer cold," Rosie said suddenly.

Hazel frowned. "You look right as rain. And you've had two pieces of icebox cake."

"Well, I feel something coming on. And I'm sure you've got family obligations. You think Rik would let Miranda help out if I was laid up?"

Hazel snorted. "You know as well as I do he'll eat at the Cattleman's Club and let dust bunnies run wild through his bedroom before he'd ask her."

Rosie grinned. "I figured on doing the asking. Surely she wouldn't say no to me, would she?"

Miranda was getting ready for bed when Rosie's call came. She was taken aback by the hoarseness in Rosie's voice and the hacking cough that came every few words.

"If you could run the sweeper and make sure something's fixed for Rik's dinner," Rosie asked in a near-whisper, "I could stay at home and rest tomorrow. A day in bed, and I'll be fine. If there was anyone else, I wouldn't ask."

Miranda agreed to drop by the next afternoon without any hesitation. During her recent stay at the ranch, Rosie had refused to let her earn her keep. This was her chance to pay back the kindness both the housekeeper and Rik had shown her.

Long after she'd hung up the phone, showered and climbed into bed, Miranda lay sleepless. Every time she escaped Rik's orbit, she somehow got sucked back in. Sighing, she punched her pillow, flopped over on her back and stared up at the ceiling. Maybe she ought to have a case of chicken soup delivered to Rosie in the morning, along with every cold and flu product she could find in Armont.

****

Everything went as planned the next day. She pulled up through the ranch gates about three p.m., did some quick light housekeeping and was gone by four. Rik arrived home to find a casserole in the refrigerator and a note on the counter telling him how long to cook it in the oven.

Wednesday, Rosie called him to announce that she was still under the weather. Rik drove into town to order cattle feed and pick up some replacement tools. The house looked exactly as he'd left it, and there was no note.

He made a couple of sandwiches and tossed them in a cooler with several bottles of water. He ate his lunch as he drove across a wide expanse of pasture land, stopping whenever he saw a barren patch. It was, he decided, nearly time to change grazing areas.

A text from his assistant at Domino had him heading back to the house. A hitch had developed in the negotiations between Domino and the company the firm was attempting to acquire. The new documents were being e-mailed, and he needed to review them immediately.

"Whatever that is, it smells great!" Rik walked into the kitchen, ten minutes.

Miranda turned and stiffened. "I thought you were gone."

"I was. I'm back." He walked over to the slow cooker and lifted the lid.

"Don't. You'll slow down the cooking time," Miranda scolded as she took the lid from him and put it back in place.

"Pot roast, huh."

"My mother's recipe. I'll put vegetables in the oven to roast before I leave."

Rik shook his head. "Don't worry about it. I've got work to do. Take it home with you if you like."

"You have to eat." Miranda protested.

"I hate eating alone." Rik tried for the right amount of pathos. "It makes me feel alone. I had a couple of bologna sandwiches back a while, so I'll be fine."

"You have to eat," Miranda said again, but this time the words sounded like a plea.

"Go home and don't worry about me."

She was saying "But Rik…" as he walked away, pretending not to hear. He hadn't lied. He didn't want to eat alone if he could guilt Miranda into dining with him.

In his study, with the door shut, he could faintly hear the sound of the sweeper. He heard the even fainter sound of music from the radio Rosie kept in the kitchen. The one thing he didn't hear was the noisy muffler of Miranda's car.

The sun was dipping toward the horizon when his study door opened and Miranda stepped inside.

"Everything's ready," she said.

"Put it in the freezer," he replied without looking up. "I'll have Rosie heat it back up once she's back."

A long silence. Then Miranda's voice again.

"Okay, I'll stay and eat with you. I don't feel like fixing a second meal anyway."

Rik felt like jumping up and pumping his fist in the air. She sounded reluctant, but she'd caved. That was an excellent sign.

He lifted his eyes to meet hers.

"I am hungry," he said, "but I don't want to impose on you. You need your personal time."

"A half hour won't kill me," Miranda replied, a snap in her voice. Rik decided not to push any further.

The food was excellent, and he was starving. Cooking was one of the things they'd never discussed, and he was impressed by her culinary skills.

"Go on home. I'll take care of the dishes." Rik started to gather up their plates and silverware. "The dishwasher's acting up, but it won't take me long to do these by hand."

"I'll wash, you dry." Miranda suggested. Rik began running the dishwater as she took care of the leftovers, hoping this impromptu domesticity didn't break their bargain.

He needed to call Rosie tonight and see how she was feeling. He couldn't remember the last time she'd missed a day. Now she'd been in bed for two straight, which made him wonder whether she had something more serious than the cold she claimed. He'd check on her in the morning. She was a stubborn woman, but between her husband and himself, maybe they could convince her a visit to the doctor wouldn't kill her.

Working together, he and Miranda made quick work of the few dishes. All too soon for his liking, Miranda was digging through her purse for her keys.

"Leaving already?"

She looked up in surprise at the wistful note in Rik's voice. "I thought you had urgent work to do."

"Yeah. But it's a nice night, and we could sit in the garden and talk."

"What about?" Rik cringed at the wary tone of her voice.

"Whatever." He tried to sound reassuring. "Anything but water rights and the price of cattle feed."

Miranda laughed. "Are you saying I'm boring?"

"No, I'm saying there are more exciting things. Like how you got in this line of work, and what you'll do when you leave here."

By the time they'd walked the length of the garden and back, Rik had discovered there was a lot more to Miranda than there had been to Randi. When she was eighteen, all she'd wanted was to leave Michigan, settle down in a city where the bright lights always shone, and find a way to become rich and famous. The birth of her daughter had made her take a second look at her plans, and she'd decided to pursue her interest in biology. From that had come a degree in natural sciences, and then a job as a park naturalist.

"When this position came along, I decided there was something to be said about the security of a government job," she confessed. "So I applied, got hired and I love it. I'm kind of a 'float' person, taking one assignment or another, which means it's never boring."

She stopped, aware of how long she'd been talking. "Tell me about you now. Do you ever regret having stayed here on the ranch?"

Rik's voice held an unexpected bitterness. "I didn't stay a second longer than I had to. When I came back from Sacramento and told my father I was leaving on the morning train, he cussed me out. He told me that I'd stay until I paid off every cent I owed him for room and board after I finished high school–and I did. I worked for the same basic wages as the hired hands until I cleared the debt, and then cashed in bonds my grandmother left me and got on the first bus out of town. I eventually wound up in a crappy job in Chicago, learned all I could there, got a better job and kept going up."

"But you're back here."

Rik laughed bitterly. "Even dead, my dad pulls the strings. He left Mom totally clueless. My brother was supposed to take over, but he cut out as soon it got hard. As soon as I get this place back in shape, I'm hiring someone to take over and I'm leaving again. This time for good."

He fell silent, staring out toward the moonlight that illuminated the far mountains. Miranda touched his face in a gentle caress of compassion. "I'm sorry."

"Don't be." He captured her hand in his and turned to her in the half-dark. "If I hadn't returned, I wouldn't have met you again. You've always been an enchantress, my love, but you're so much, much more now."

His words, so quietly spoken, unleashed the flood of emotions Miranda had dammed up for so long. Sadness for the pain he'd faced. Pride in his accomplishments. Grief that after swearing she'd share his life, she hadn't trusted him. She raised her face, tears shimmering in her eyes, and whispered, "If only we could go back and start again."

"It's not too late." He pulled her to him, his arms gentle yet possessive. "I didn't know how much I missed you until I saw you again, and now I don't know how I can ever let you leave me a second time."

Miranda pulled away, tears escaping in twin trails down her cheeks. "We can't revive the past, Rik. We've both moved on. It can never be the way you want."

He grabbed her arms and forced her to face him. "Yes, it can. What is there to stop us? If it's your daughter, we can work it out. Dammit, I love you and I know you love me. I can give you a good life, you and your daughter both."

"You don't understand…" her voice trailed off.

"We can work it out," he insisted. "Ten years ago, you wanted to live some place where life was vibrant and exciting. I can give you that. You'll love San Francisco. You quit your job, I'll cut back my hours and we'll travel wherever you want. How would you like a month in Europe as a honeymoon?"

"Are you crazy?" Miranda twisted away, her voice rising. "You can't possibly expect me to simply walk away from the past ten years and my career. I already have a life, remember? Sorry if it can't compare with yours, but it makes me happy."

Rik lashed out, wounded by her rejection. "If you're still carrying a torch for the loser who knocked you up, you're going to spend your life alone. If the guy wouldn't stand by you when you were pregnant, why stick around waiting for him to show back up? I'm offering you a real life with me, not the dream one you're hoping for."

"Shut up." Miranda shoved past him, nearly blinded by tears of pain. Her small hands were curled into fists, and her muscles tightened as she fought for self-control. "You don't know anything."

"I know I was wrong and we need to talk about the past," Rik said, his voice cold. "But we won't. You'll run away again. You're good at that, aren't you? Maybe I've got it all wrong and you walked out on your lover, not caring whether your kid had a father or not.

Miranda whirled, rage building inside her. She began to shake, her heart pounding, and curled her hands into fists. She fought back tears of anger, struggling to control the ten years of sacrifice and worry single parenthood had brought her. "Brittani's going to be eleven in March, Rik," she yelled. "Do the math! Who the hell do you think her father is?"

The words hung in the still night as she ran pell-mell to her car, desperate to be alone.

****

The sun was past its zenith the next day when Miranda finally called it quits. She was hot, she was tired, and by now she must have counted every creature twice over. She wanted to blame her fierce headache on the heat, but she knew it was the result of too little sleep and too many self-recriminations. How could she have told Rik he was Brittani's father? She had intended to take that secret to her grave.

If only he hadn't said he loved her. For a brief and exhilarating moment, it had been enough to know that his feelings for her had never died. No, it had started earlier, with his bitter account of being trapped by his father's demands. At long last, she knew why he hadn't shown up at the train station, the reason for his broken vow.

"There's a seat by me."

Those five words had started it all. She'd been traveling by train to Sacramento from Detroit to visit her college roommate at the end of her freshman year. Train travel was supposed to be scenic and romantic, and she had plenty of time.

Rik had been on his way to take a computer short-course for ranchers. She supposed it was money that had made his tight-fisted father decided Rik should go by rail. At the time, she gave all the credit to fate.

His accent and those gorgeous blue eyes had tempted her to take the seat. By the time the train reached its final destination, she'd found so much more about him that appealed to her. His self-assuredness. The way he made her feel there was no woman on the train but her. The feelings he aroused in her, as if this was the man destiny had created for her.

Those three weeks in Sacramento had been an enchanted time. She spent the daytime hours with her friend while Rik was in class. The evenings they spent together, taking in the sights, finding quiet tables for two in restaurants they discovered and walking hand-in-hand down the city streets. Every one of those nights ended in Rik's hotel bed, where she gave him her virginity and eagerly accepted his tutoring in the art of love.

He left two days before her, leaving her a red rose to remind her of his love and a promise to meet her at the train station in Detroit a week later. She'd met every incoming train that day, still there long after the last eastbound train had arrived. She'd called a friend for a ride home, still believing Rik would be come to her.

Two months later, she finally told her parents she was pregnant. She expected them to turn their backs. But they supported her, financially and emotionally, accepting her decision not to name the father.

Her life had come full circle. Rik had offered her his eternal love again, but she was no longer a starry-eyed virgin. She was a woman with a child whose needs came first.

Sighing, she packed up her things and headed back to the cabin. She'd pop some ibuprofen, rest until the headache faded and then work on her reports.

She'd just swallowed the pills and slipped off her boots when a knock came on the door. She looked out the window and saw Rik.

"Go away!" She winced at the pain her shout caused in her head.

"I've got to talk to you. This is important."

"Go away!" she yelled again. "We have nothing to talk about."

"It's about our daughter," he called back.

Miranda flung the door open and glared at him. "Brittani is mine. Her birth certificate says father unknown. I'll fight you in court if you try to interfere."

"I'm not here to talk about taking her away. It's something totally different."
The frown between Rik's eyes worried her. Why else would he be here?

"She's hurt, isn't she?" Miranda dropped onto the porch step, her mind creating an image of her daughter in bandages in a hospital bed or sporting a cast on her arm.

"She's fine." Rik knelt beside her. "I swear. Frank's been trying to get hold of you all morning, and he called the ranch to see if you were there. I told him I'd find you and give you the message myself."

"Just tell me!"

"Your mother had emergency heart surgery this morning. Frank talked to your dad, who said she's doing really well. He said not to worry; she should be home in a few days."

"Brittani must be scared to death." Miranda grabbed her cell phone from her back pack and swore. "Damn thing is dead. Can I use yours?"

"Sure." He handed it over. "Frank said to tell you he'll authorize three days of compassionate leave if you want to go back to Michigan."

"Oh God." Miranda held the phone without dialing, conflicted. She wanted nothing more than to sit by her mother's side at the hospital, to be there for her father, to tuck her daughter into bed. Yet could she trust Frank?

She closed her eyes, took a deep breath and decided there was only one choice.

Home.

"Do you know which airlines fly out of Denver?" she asked as she punched in her parents' familiar number. "I need to get the first flight heading to Detroit."

"How do wheels up in an hour sound?"

"You have that much pull?"

"No, my own plane. It actually is ranch property, but I'm the only one with a pilot's license now."

In less than that hour, they were taxiing down the runway of the small airport outside Armont. The flight was smoother than she'd expected, but it seemed interminably long. When the plane touched down and stopped, she was ready to jump out and find her family before the engine cut off. First, though, she turned to Rik, her face solemn.

He apparently anticipated her request, for he spoke before she could.

"Don't worry," he said. "I'm your pilot, nothing more. Go see your daughter now."

Rik walked to the airport office to make arrangements to hangar the plane, allowing her time for a private reunion with her family. He held back when he spied Miranda standing beside her father, Brittani's arms tight around her waist.

"Good flight?" Bill Coulsen walked over and grabbed Rik's hand. "I appreciate your bringing my girl like this. I know it will do her mother a world of good to see her, and it's already been good for our little one."

*He knows.*

Rik was as sure of that as he was his own name. He could tell by the speculative look in the older man's eyes, and by the handshake that was as much challenge as welcome. He understood why when Brittani looked up from her mother and shyly said, "Hello."

Rik's heart stopped. Gazing at his daughter's face was like looking in a family album. Her eyes were hazel, instead of the blue of the Hallowells, but she had the heart-shaped face of his mother and his father's high cheekbones. He would have recognized her as his even if Miranda hadn't said a word.

He glanced at Miranda and saw the plea in her eyes. He nodded slightly, acknowledging her unspoken request for his silence. The frown between her eyes lessened.

It was almost exactly eleven years since he'd pressed a red rose in her hand on the train platform in Sacramento and promised her nothing could keep them apart. But he'd let his bullheaded pride do it, his foolish belief that he had to pay off his father or lose his respect. That stubbornness had cost him the chance to be this child's father.

"Is that your suitcase, Mom?" The little girl pointed to a flowered bag on the baggage carousel, and ran off to retrieve it. Miranda took advantage of her temporary absence to murmur, "You're not going to say anything, are you?"

"No," Rik whispered back. "We've got to do a whole lot of talking first. You, me, and your parents."

Miranda barely had time to whisper a grateful "thanks" before her daughter reappeared pulling the wheeled suitcase. When Rik suggested checking into the airport hotel, her father didn't protest.

"Call me tonight." Miranda slipped her cell number into Rik's hand before he went to catch a hotel shuttle. "I'll...we'll..."

"See your mother, take care of your daughter and don't worry about me. You know where I'll be if you need me."

Miranda watched him walk away, boot heels clacking on the tile floor, already missing his strength. She knew her father would insist on a talk tonight, one they should have had a long time ago.

It was nearly midnight before she and her father settled down at the kitchen table with coffee mugs. Miranda felt like a kid again, trapped under father's stare like a butterfly on a collection board.

"Does Hallowell know he's Brit's father?" Bill's gaze was firm on his daughter's face as he blurted out the question. "More importantly, what does he intend to do about it?"

Miranda's shoulders slumped. "I don't know. He just found out yesterday, and quite honestly, I think he's still a little stunned."

"Your mother and I assumed it was Brian. I was pretty happy when he moved to Atlanta. I couldn't see him without wanting to pound him."

Miranda swallowed hard. Confession time was here, and she needed to clear the air before her mother came home.

"Brian and I never…"

Bill reached out and covered her hand with his. "Honey, it's none of my business what happened between you and Brian. I want to know more about this Hallowell fellow. No one, not even him, is going to hurt you or your little girl.

"I've been pretty frugal all my life, and I've got some stock I can sell to pad out what's in the bank. You do what you have to do for your future and hers, and don't worry about paying for lawyers and such. Your mother and I will take care of that."

Miranda's eyes welled up. "Dad, that's so sweet. But Rik doesn't want to hurt Brittani, either."

Her father studied her shrewdly. "I don't know if he's sincere or just saying the right thing. You wear your heart on your sleeve, always have. You have feelings for him, I can tell. Don't do anything foolish, you hear me?"

"Dad, I'm almost thirty years old; I think I can take care of myself." She offered a wan smile. "Let's not get lawyers involved unless we have to, okay? Right now all I want is a shower and a bed. I'm wiped out."

Before Miranda sought oblivion, she called Rik. He was pleasant and concerned, with none of the emotion his voice had held in the ranch garden the night before.

"I'm glad your mom's doing well," he said after she gave him a brief update. "I think it's good for her to see you, and good for you to see your own daughter."

She was quite aware that he said "your" and not "our," a distinction that relieved the worry building in her since talking with her father the night before. *If* Rik forced the issue, *if* he insisted on visitation, *if* lawyers got involved–all those ifs were for a later time.

"Thank you for making it possible," she said. "You'll never know what it means to me. Mom should be able to come tomorrow, so I'll book a flight for the next day."

"No need. We can stay as long as you need."

"I can't ask you to wait for me. The ranch, your job–that's all back West."

"I have a messenger bag full of ranch records that may take a magician to figure out. Having a couple of days away from everyone and everything to start sorting it out is exactly what I need."

"Your room? Is it okay?"

Rik chuckled. "The hotel has a king bed with a great mattress, Wi-Fi and a restaurant with decent food. Trust me, I'll be fine."

"Well, if you're sure…"

"I'm sure. Now go to bed. I can sleep in come morning, but I suspect you'll have a girl bouncing on your bed come daylight."

After mutual goodbyes, Miranda cut the call with a lighter heart than when she'd dialed. She felt as if a truce had been called for the time being, even though absolutely nothing was settled.

\*\*\*\*

After taking Brittani to school, she spent the next morning preparing the house for her mother's homecoming. She changed the beds, mopped floors and washed windows. With Brittani in tow, she made a trip to the grocery store and stopped by the florist's shop to pick up a fresh arrangement for her mother.

Trying to sound casual, she said as they drove back home, "You know your grandparents aren't going to be able to take you places like they have been. Promise you won't get upset when they just want to stay home."

"Oh, Mom." In drama-queen fashion, Brittani rolled her eyes and sighed heavily. "I am not a little kid. Tara's slumber party is Friday, and Gramps knows all about it. Next week is Girl Scout camp, remember?" She tipped her head and looked speculatively at her mother. "Maybe your boyfriend could take Tara and me in his plane before you go back to work. That would be sweet."

Miranda forced a smile and said, "Honey, Mr. Hallowell isn't my boyfriend. I met him through my work."

Brittani giggled.

"Right, Mom. He has nothing to do but fly you around." She bit her lower lip and looked at her mother. "You know, Mom, if you want a boyfriend, it's okay with me. Tara's mom has a boyfriend and he's really cool. He's got a red Hummer and he's going to take us all for a ride after her party. But that's not as cool as having a plane."

Miranda laughed. "I'll work on finding someone with a yacht and a private island. Would you like that?"

"Yeah," came the enthusiastic reply. "It would rock to have my next birthday party on a yacht."

Miranda sighed and shook her head. She had hoped her daughter would stay a little girl a bit longer, but Brittani was growing up fast. Before long, she'd be old enough to worry about her own boyfriends rather than her mother's.

"Wow, Mom, look!" Brittani pointed at a fast food restaurant's sign. "They've got the new Cuddle Kitten collection already!"

Miranda relaxed. Thank heavens for the little stuffed creatures. She'd talk about Cuddle Kittens all day long if she never had to discuss men in general, and Rik Hallowell in particular, with Brittani again.

## Chapter Ten

Bill Coulson's heart beat a heavy tattoo as he walked down the hallway to Rik's hotel room. They should have had this talk last night. Hell, they should have had this talk years ago. He'd have flown to Colorado or the ends of the earth if he'd known about Hallowell.

He and Mary had longed for another child, but God had only given them Miranda. Maybe if they'd had more than one chick to worry about, he would have handled things better when she came home from college, looking bad and crying the instant she walked in the door.

He stopped in an alcove that held the ice and pop machines to compose himself. Stress over Mary's surgery and the turmoil of seeing Hallowell walk in, his resemblance to Brittani so strong, brought back memories he'd hoped had been lost forever. Miranda's tearful confession that she was five months pregnant and not going back to school after Thanksgiving break. Mary's silent sobs that became tearful recriminations as he held her in the privacy of their bedroom. His daughter's refusal to tell them who the father was.

He'd been ready to drive over to Brian's house and beat the truth out of him. If a boy was old enough to get a girl pregnant, he was old enough to handle it like a man. That's what his own father had told him when Bill started feeling the hormonal stirrings of a teenager.

Mary's tears had stopped him. That and his innate knowledge that the worst thing Miranda could do was get married to Brian or anyone else. She was too young and inexperienced; he didn't want her to carry the burden of a divorce before she turned twenty-one.

"Excuse me." The soft interruption by a girl with a dollar brought him back to the moment. Stepping back into the hall, he started toward Room 227 once again.

Rik opened the door wearing faded jeans and a chambray shirt, a cup of takeout coffee in his hand.

"Mr. Hallowell..." Bill began after the door shut behind him.

"Rik. Please."

"Okay." He gathered his courage and started again.

"I've spent the last ten years blaming another kid for my girl getting pregnant. Miranda's done a good job of building a life for herself and that little girl, and I don't intend to let anyone tear it down."

"I don't want my daughter to suffer either." Rik's quiet words hung in the room. "We made mistakes, Miranda and I, but now we have to decide what's best for Brittani together."

"My daughter's been making those decisions alone for the past ten years, and she's done one helluva fine job of it. She doesn't need help from someone like you."

Rik stared into the man's belligerent eyes and held back his own temper.

"If I'd known about Miranda's pregnancy, Brittani would have been born with the Hallowell name and been raised by us both," he finally said. "The past can't be changed. It's over and done with. What we're discussing is their future."

"One my girls already have planned out." Bill's hands clenched and his jaw tightened. "I don't know what you've been doing out there in Colorado together, and I don't want to know. That's your business. Brittani, on the other hand, is my business, and I'll spend every dime I have to make sure she stays where she belongs."

Rik took deep breaths and counted to ten. Coulsen spoke from fear, not hate. He knew that. Still, a man could only take so much.

"You're right. It is none of your business. I intend to provide for Brittani now that I know about her, in any way her mother will let me which I hope comes to more than money."

"Miranda knows what's best for the two of them," he went on. "Neither of us have the right to tell her what to do."

Bill's face tightened, blood rising in his face. Rik decided it was time to end the conversation.

"When I leave, Brittani will still know me only as her mother's friend. I trust you and your wife to also respect your daughter's ability to manage her own life. Now I suggest you leave."

He reached for the knob and yanked the door open, waving his hand in an invitation for the older man to leave. His head ached from the tension of the last five minutes, and his stomach felt as if he'd swallowed a bowling ball. Crazy as it seemed, he wanted to talk to Miranda now. He needed to hear her voice, for her to say there was room in Britanni's life for them both. Most of all he wanted to know why Miranda had told him about their child after all these years. Had it truly been accidental? Was she hoping they might become a family?

The questions nagged at him even as he tried to concentrate on the profit and loss statements he'd brought along. As darkness descended, he gave up and dialed Miranda's cell phone. After a short conversation, she'd agreed to meet him in the hotel lounge after Brittani was asleep.

Rik's heart caught when she slipped into the chair across from him. The stress of the last two days showed in the slump of her shoulders and dark circles lining her eyes. She fidgeted with the buttons of her polo shirt as she greeted him.

"How's your mom?" he asked.

"Pretty good, thanks to the pain pills. Dad looked so rough when they got home that I was afraid something had gone wrong and he wasn't telling me. But when I called her doctor, I was reassured. She should be as good as new in a month or so."

Rik hesitated, wondering how to phrase his next question.

"Do you think it would be easier if your daughter came back with you for a week or two? She can stay with Rosie while you're working."

"You've got be kidding."

Rik was still processing her blunt refusal when she started to soften her comment.

"She has things she has to do here," Miranda said. "She has friends here, and I think my mom will do better if she has Brittani around."

He noticed the small trembling in her hands as she accepted the cup of coffee the server brought and realized she might have made the wrong assumption.

"She's not going to know anything," he insisted. "At her age, it will be an adventure."

"One she won't want to end. She's ten. Offer her a pony and a puppy, and she'll be eating out of your hand. Tell her you're her father, and she'll be ready to stay."

When tears welled in her eyes, Rik wanted to hold her and tell her everything would be all right. Wanted to, but couldn't. The foundation on which he'd built his adult life was crumbling.

"Tell you what," he said, "we'll leave everything as it is. Your daughter stays with your folks, we go back to the life we were living and that's that."

"Like it's that easy." She blinked and offered a passable smile.

"There is one thing, though. Your father came to see me today."

****

"Oh, lord." Miranda stared down at the table. She had been half afraid Dad would do something, but she'd talked herself into believing he'd let her handle things for once.

She should have known better. Letting things take their natural course had never been Dad's style. He was the one who'd go charging into the principal's office if she got a grade he didn't think she deserved. The time she'd gotten a speeding ticket, it had been all she and her mother could do to keep him from going to court to tell the judge that his little girl would never break the law.

"How bad was it?" She braced herself for Rik's answer.

"We both got a little testy, but no one threw a punch."

"That's a relief. Let me guess: he told you to stay away, that he could take care of us both."

"More or less. It was a short conversation, but I assured him that now that I know I'm a father, I'll live up to my responsibilities."

She offered a wry smile. "I'm sure that went over well."

"Better than when I told him he has no business telling you how to run your life."

"Yet you sit here with no bruises and no broken bones. I'm very proud of my dad."

Rik took her hands in his and studied her for a moment.

"I meant what I said. If it was up to me, Brittani would know already that she has a dad who is thrilled to claim that title. But the choice is yours. You get to decide when to tell her and what to tell her. In the meantime, I intend to set up a trust fund for her and provide support payments. I swear I'll make up for all those things I should have been doing."

Miranda itched to erase the frown lines between his eyes, to ease the hurt she saw there. All these years, she thought she'd done what was best for all of them. She'd justified her actions as a way to protect Brittani, and her own heart. Had she been wrong all this time? She took a deep breath and began to speak.

"Part of the reason I am who I am now is because you weren't there. My parents have always been protective, and it would have been easy to let you take over my life and my decisions. Having Brittani on my own, creating a life in her best interest and not mine, changed me for the better."

"If I'd been on that train instead of stuck paying off my dad, would you have married me?" he asked.

Miranda smiled. "Of course. I was crazy over you. I wouldn't have hesitated."

"So why not marry me now?"

She stared at him.

"You're kidding, right?"

"I'm serious. I want you as my wife."

"For me, or because we made a child?" Her voice was small and shaky.

"Both. I'm beginning to realize how hollow my life is. You know that saying about money not buying happiness? I've learned that firsthand." He sighed.

"I want you, Miranda, in every sense of the word. I want a family, too. You and Brittani there when I get up in the morning and when I go to bed at night."

"Rik, I…" she pushed away from the table. "I'll be right back."

She stumbled away from the table and into the ladies' room. For so long she'd dreamed Rik would come and make her world right again. Eventually that dream faded, new ones taking its place.

But his proposal was tempting. Brittani deserved a father. She'd asked once, when she was about six, why she didn't have a daddy. Apparently she'd been satisfied with Miranda's explanation, because she had never inquired again. Still, the absence of one would become more difficult for her as she grew into a teenager, then an adult. If she decided as a young woman to find her father, would she blame Miranda for hiding the truth?

Miranda paced the small room, her heart urging her to say yes and her mind cautioning her to take it slow. When two giggling, tipsy twenty-somethings came in, she left, still torn by Rik's second proposal in a week.

Rik's face was a study in neutrality when she rejoined him.

"It's no, isn't it?" He spoke before she could. "It's okay. I understand."

"It's...I don't know what." Miranda surprised herself with her answer. "A beautiful, smart, funny child came out of our incredible first love, and I'll always be grateful for Brittani. You'll adore her, of course, everyone does. Yet raising a child, having her as the most important thing in your life...that takes more than love."

"I know."

"No, you don't. Until you've lived through all those moments, big and small, that connect you, there's no way to understand. The most important thing in my life is our child, and I refuse to be rushed into a decision."

"I'm not rushing you."

Miranda took a deep breath. Two back-to-back proposals certainly didn't translate into "take your time." There was so much he'd missed, such as Brittani's first steps and her terrible twos. The first time she said "Mama" and the arguments over baths and bedtimes.

"I can't do this now," she said. "Yeah, we need to talk about the future but not tonight. Not when I'm worried and not thinking clearly. I hope you understand."

She picked up her purse and slid from the booth. Her life had been so neat and orderly a few weeks ago, and now it was one big mess. She had obligations. Her mother needed her, and her daughter.

"I'm not pressuring you. Things are complicated, yeah, but sooner or later, we have to make some decisions." Rik hastily stood as well, pulling some bills from his wallet which he tossed on the table."

Miranda didn't protest, although she kept distance between them.

"Over there." She pointed at the car she'd borrowed from her father.

An awkward moment came as she unlocked the door, prepared to slide in. Rik grabbed her hand and held her back as if he was afraid she'd disappear if he let go.

"Rik, I have to go," she whispered, tugging her hand away. "Back to my family now and back to my job tomorrow. Call and tell me what time to be at the airport."

"I don't want you to leave." He stepped away, tucking his hands in his pockets. "It's stupid, I know, but I feel that if we say goodbye now, I'll never see you again."

Miranda gave a wry half-smile. "Still have a problem with trust issues, I see. Go to bed. I'll see you tomorrow."

From behind the steering wheel, she watched him walk across the dark lot toward the beckoning bright lights of the motel. He had every reason to hate her, to use his money and connections to force a custody battle. Yet the goodness that first drew her to him was still there.

\*\*\*\*

Brittani's shout woke her the next morning, a bright, chipper voice calling, "Mom! Grandpa says get down here because pancakes are ready!"

After Brittani chowed down her breakfast and ran upstairs to see her grandmother, there was no noise except the clatter of silverware on plates as Miranda and her father finished their meal. As they drank a second cup of coffee, Bill said, "You went to see him last night, didn't you?"

The words sounded like an accusation, not an inquiry.

Miranda met his gaze squarely. "Yes."

"Did you sleep with him?"

"Dad!" Miranda felt her face get warm. "It's none of your business, but the answer's no."

Bill shrugged. "Maybe you should. Get this guy out of your system so things can get back to the way they ought to be."

Miranda chose her words with care. She didn't want to hurt her father, but he had to understand her feelings.

"If things were as they ought to be, Rik and I would be married, and Brittani would have a sister or brother by now. If you mean the way things used to be, you'd better realize everything's different. Rik is a fact of life. He's Brittani's father, and you'll have to accept that."

She picked up the dishes and headed for the sink. "Since Mom's okay, I need to return to work. Rik's flying us back today."

"Brittani, too?" Bill's voice was tight.

Miranda turned. "Rik asked me to consider it."

"Please don't take her." Bill's eyes filled with unaccustomed tears. "I can't stand to lose the both of you."

"Dad, you're not losing either of us. I told him no. I'll be back before Labor Day, when this assignment is over. I'll take Brittani and we'll go house hunting. Just as I planned."

She smiled and recited an oath from her childhood days, fingers slashing across her chest. "Cross my heart and hope to die."

Her dad laughed. "Go to your mom now. I'd rather you not say a word about Hallowell. I thought it best if we wait till she's stronger to bring it up."

"Okay," Miranda said, "but don't wait too long. Brittani *is* going to meet her father." She held up a finger in warning, cutting off her father's protest. "And that decision will be made by Rik and me, and no one else. Promise?"

Her father nodded.

"You know I love you, Dad," Miranda said, kissing his cheek. "But I am a grown-up now."

"Not to me. You'll always be my little chick." His soft words stayed with her after she left the room, an unexpected reminder of the love between daddies and their little girls.

## Chapter Eleven

The sun glanced off the small plane's windshield as Rik eased it down on the runway of the small airstrip outside Armont. Miranda was relieved that the flight had been smooth and their conversation had been minimal and inconsequential.

Miranda was exhausted, both physically and emotionally. She'd lain awake wrestling with regrets from the past and fear for the future. She wanted a quiet, uncomplicated life. Rik's was anything but that. How could she fit into his lifestyle? How could Brittani fit into his life?

She was better off without a father than living with a workaholic whose home was an extension of his office. Miranda had lived through that as Dad built his law practice, pretending to understand why her father missed landmark events in her life. She needed someone who understood how short and precious the years were between welcoming a baby into a family and watching that child walk out the door as a self-sufficient adult.

"You hungry?" They were on the edge of town when Rik interrupted her circular thoughts. "I could use a burger."

Miranda glanced at the clock on the dash. Nearly three p.m., and the last she'd eaten was a bowl of cereal with Brittani eight hours earlier. No wonder she felt like she could eat a cow.

Miranda nodded. "I could handle that. I suppose you want to stop at the Cattleman's Club."

"Beats the diner by a mile."

"Anything beats the diner, even my cooking."

She caught a glimpse of Junie Delacroix sashaying into the club as Rik pulled into an empty parking place. The reality of being back in Armont hit her like a slap. She had about thirty seconds to decide what to do next.

"The food's not as good down the road, but the company may be better," Rik said, letting her know he'd also noticed Junie. "I figure you'd like peace and quiet after the last couple of days."

"No way! After two major conversations with my dad in 24 hours, Junie's nothing more than a fly in the kitchen, buzzing around but not doing any damage. Besides, I'm starving."

"Well, then, let's get a cheeseburger."

Heads turned as they walked into the restaurant. Several of the men called greetings to Rik, who slid his hand against the small of Miranda's back as they headed for a booth at the back. Was the attention was because she and Rik had been gone together or because Junie had made her presence in the place obvious?

"Missed you guys." The waitress plopped a basket of tortilla chips down on the table and waited for their drink order. "Rosie said you'd been called away."

"Miranda got lonesome for her daughter, so I flew her to Michigan," Rik said easily. "I had some business to take care of so we killed two birds with one stone."

"You've got a daughter?" The waitress brightened up. "So do I. Three, actually. You'll have to bring in a picture sometime. I love kids. If the old man and I could afford it, I'd have a houseful."

"Me, too," Rik murmured so only Miranda could hear. "I can afford a dozen, but I need a Mommy for them first."

Miranda smiled sweetly and said, "I'm sure you can find a volunteer," nodding in Junie's direction. Avoiding Rik's grimace, she slid out to pop some quarters in the jukebox.

"Looking for a special song for the two of you?" The question came from Junie, naturally walking over to lean against the neon-lit jukebox and study the selections. "Here's a good one. It's about a guy who marries the wrong woman and spends his life regretting it. Oh, and here's another one you might like. It's about this woman who steals another woman's man, and he breaks her heart in return."

Miranda fought back the impulse to bop Junie in the nose. Ignoring her as much as possible, she punched in songs at random before returning to slide into the booth next to Rik.

"She is such a witch," she muttered, leaning toward him so no one could overhear. "I cannot believe you stooped to dating her in the first place."

Rik tipped her face toward him. "I love it when you're jealous."

"I am not jealous," she retorted. "You'd better let go. She's watching to see if we kiss."

"Hate to disappoint my audience," he said, dropping his lips to Miranda's for a brief moment. He chuckled as she pulled away, scooting slightly down the seat to put distance between them.

"Play with fire, you're going to get burned," he cautioned. "One of these days, it's going to get too hot for you to handle."

Somehow, Miranda managed to get through lunch without punching out either Rik or Junie. That woman, she'd never like. Rik, she was trying hard not to like too much. Aggravating as he could be sometimes, she missed him when he wasn't around.

She was glad to be dropped off at her little cabin, and thankful for the quiet refuge it provided. Her ordinarily calm life was too full of complications. She needed to be alone to sort through everything that had happened in the last week.

She sat on the old wooden rocker on the porch and stared toward the setting sun. Her life was one big mess. If she'd known the emotional cost of that three-week affair, she might have ignored Rikky's invitation to join him. How she could have deluded herself into thinking that particular chicken would never come home to roost, she didn't know.

The sharp ring of her cell phone startled her. Her father's voice boomed across the line.

"I just wanted to make sure he got you home all right, kiddo."

"Rik is an excellent pilot," she answered, stressing the name.

"I don't doubt that," her father said. "He strikes me as the kind of person who's better with machines than people."

"Dad, don't do this," Miranda warned. "It's been ten years, so it's a little too late for resentment now."

She held her breath during the brief silence that followed. Was he going to hang up? Or were they going to have an adult, father-to-daughter conversation at last?

"I worry about you," he finally said. "I'd feel better if you were closer to home."

"You mean you'd feel better if Rik was farther away," she corrected gently. "I'm a big girl, Dad, and you have to accept that I need to make my own decisions. Rik and I have a lot of talking to do, about a lot more things than Brittani."

There was nothing but silence on the other end, a pause that stretched so long Miranda wondered if the call had dropped. Eventually her father resumed speaking.

"You're right," he said, his voice choppy. "Your decisions are your own. I'm afraid you'll make another mistake, not looking below the surface. He must be something to have blinded you that way."

"No more, Dad." Miranda fought against the anger surging inside her. "Let's talk about something else. Like how Mom's doing."

Her dad began to fill her in on her mother's continued recuperation and Brittani's plans for the next few days. Miranda breathed a silent sigh of relief. The last thing she wanted was get in a long-distance argument with her father that would leave them both upset.

They'd had one of those arguments before she'd gone to Sacramento to visit her friend. He thought she was too young to go alone; she had insisted she was old enough to run her own life. No wonder he was concerned about her now. She'd certainly proved him right back then.

She was even more conflicted after they'd said goodbye. Her father sounded resigned, like he expected something terrible to happen. She knew what he thought, that she'd let emotion cloud her better judgment. Maybe, she decided as she went into the cabin to make a grilled cheese sandwich, he was right. Maybe she needed to let go of everything until she was back in Michigan and far from the source of her worries.

****

Clouds hung low in the sky the next morning, heavy with incipient rain. Miranda pulled on her waterproof boots and stuck her rain poncho in the car. She'd worked in a downpour before; rain couldn't stop her.

She was about ready to call it a day, even though it was only mid-afternoon, when she saw Rik's battered truck headed for her, swaying in the rutted road. He stopped beside her and stepped out.

"Frank called to see if we could meet with some ranchers over toward Pueblo," he said without preamble. "I told I was free, and he said he you would be, too. Pick you up about six?"

"A good afternoon to you, too," she said tartly. "Your day is going well, I hope?"

He had the grace to look abashed. He didn't speak, though, just stood with his hat cocked back on his head, one foot on the truck's running board, waiting for her answer.

She sighed. "Okay, fine. But I'll pick you up. My turn to drive, remember?"

When she pulled in front of the ranch house a little before six p.m., Rosie came out to greet her instead of Rik.

"He's out moving steers," she said with a shrug. "Come into the kitchen and have a cup of coffee while I finish the dishes. How's your mother?"

They'd exhausted that topic, as well as numerous others, by the time Rik stalked into the kitchen, slamming the door behind him and muttering, "Give me ten minutes and we're out of here."

Wiping her hands on a dish towel, Rosie dropped into the chair opposite Miranda, folded her hands in front of her on the table and said, "So give. He's been curt and grumpy since he got back. What is going on between the two of you?"

"Nothing. I swear," Miranda said, making an X across her heart. "It's probably the weather."

Rosie snorted. "It's probably the combination of you and that Junie. He wants you and you won't give him the time of day. Junie wants him so bad she can taste it, because he's the best catch around here. I'm still trying to figure it all out."

Miranda laughed. "I'm open and shut, Rosie. My priorities are my daughter, my parents and my job, in that order. Romance takes a back burner to all of that."

Rosie snorted again. "Tell me another one, young lady. I've seen the way you look at him when you don't think anyone's around, and how he moons after you. I'm not fooled."

Miranda immediately jumped to her own defense. "Okay, sometimes I think about what it would be like to do more than ride to meetings with him. It's only because I'm alone out here, and he's around all the time. Hormones and togetherness. That's it, nothing more."

Miranda was saved from further grilling by the surprisingly quick appearance of Rik, buttoning his shirt as he came into the kitchen grousing about the cattle. Acknowledging her with a curt nod, he said, "I'm ready" and headed toward her car without another word. Miranda exchanged looks and shrugged shoulders with Rosie before following him out the door.

Rik stayed uncommunicative all the way to the meeting. Miranda had no idea what was eating him, and she wasn't about to ask. Work, probably. He'd been texting back and forth the whole time. Or maybe it was some problem with the ranch.

Within minutes of arriving at the meeting hall, Rik turned on his usual charm, slapping one guy on the back and asking the next how his crops were doing while ignoring Miranda the whole time. She resolutely threw herself into the same grip-and-grin activity, introducing herself and finally getting the meeting underway only ten minutes late.

Rik's amiable mood faded as soon as the lights of town dimmed behind them. Miranda didn't try to make conversation; let him pout, if that's what he wanted. Still, it was hard to stay focused with a sullen man beside her, and so she pulled into the parking lot of the last all-night diner before Armont.

"I have to get home," he said when she announced that she needed coffee. "Get it to go and I'll drive."

"You can go in." Miranda unsnapped her seat belt and reached over to snap off his. "I don't care if you're planning a midnight powwow with your business buddies or just want to put on your jammies and go to bed. I've had enough of your mood, and we're going to talk it out right here and now, on neutral ground."

"Go get your coffee," he said again.

Miranda jumped out of the car, walked around and opened his door. "Move. I said we're going in and talk, and I mean it. I'm not above making a scene."

"Fine, then. We'll go in."

He unfolded his tall frame from the low seat and stretched, his arms reaching far above his head. He walked toward the diner, ignoring the woman beside him.

Rik held the door for Miranda and followed her to a back booth, far away from the other customers. He slid into the seat, tipped his hat back, and reached for the plastic-covered menu that stood propped up against the sugar shaker without saying a word. She resisted the temptation to sail his hat across the room to see if he'd react. She grabbed another menu instead and pretended an avid interest in the "all day, any way" breakfast menu on the back page. She muttered "hot tea, cream, no lemon," when the waitress came to take their order.

"So what's good?" Rik asked their server. "I was leaning toward the cheeseburger."

"Lots of people order it," the twenty-something answered. "Me, I like the open face roast beef sandwich."

"You've convinced me." Rik smiled as he tucked the menu away. "Tell me about the cherry pie. Is it was sweet as you?"

"I'll be back." Miranda slid out and headed for the restroom. Miranda faced herself in the mirror. Was she jealous? Maybe. Not of that girl, but of the way Rik flirted with her. Of the uncomplicated relationship they might have right now if there wasn't so much history between them. She was pretty sure Rik's proposal had been inspired by his desire to have a relationship with Brittani, but what was in it for her?

Sex, yeah. That was a given. She'd had a few dates now and again since Brittani's birth, but nothing serious. The one man she'd slept with since then hadn't had half the skill Rik had at twenty-one. She was not only ready for a man, she was long overdue. Looking back, she should have gone to bed with him when the sizzle began again, before the stakes went up. It was way too late to offer friendship with benefits now.

A rap on the door reminded her the diner had other patrons, so she quickly splashed cold water on her face and patted it dry with the rough paper towel. Her tea was at the table when she got back, served exactly as she'd ordered it.

"I ordered you a fish sandwich and fries," Rik said,

"Cod or whitefish?" Miranda asked. She'd see how good his memory was.

"Whitefish. You hate cod." He sipped his coffee, and added, "I told her to forget the catsup, since you're weird and eat mustard with your fries."

He was good, she'd give him that. He had remembered those little food idiosyncrasies for a decade. Still, things like that didn't mean all that much. Did they?

"The heat must be on in here," she said finally, watching his reaction.

He frowned. "It's eighty degrees outside. Why would they have the heat on?"

"Because you finally warmed up. You've been so cool all night I could feel frostbite setting in."

Instead of answering, Rik drained his cup and motioned to the waitress for a refill.

"Your food will be up in a moment," she assured Rik, flashing him a wide smile. "I'll get it right to you."

Miranda was right. Rik's attention had guaranteed good service, at least for him. The waitress barely noticed her. Then again, Rik might as well have been eating alone for all the attention he paid her. He even pulled out his cell phone and walked to the end of the diner to make calls while she nibbled on her sandwich. She could see him smiling and suspected the call was personal.

When he finally returned, he wiggled two fingers at the waitress who immediately showed up with the coffee pot. Once again, he was more than friendly with his new friend even as he continued to ignore Miranda.

Reminding herself she didn't care who or what he did, she waited outside as he paid the bill and came out with a phone number written on his hand.

"A souvenir?" she asked, attempting for a neutral tone. He didn't answer. Miranda felt a slow burn begin. He was busy with his cell phone, probably adding the number to his contact list.

## Chapter Twelve

"What in the world did you do to that girl?"

Rik was jolted awake by an irritated Rosie pounding on his bed's headboard with a metal spatula. She wore an apron, but he didn't smell anything cooking. She didn't look like she was about to start cooking, either.

The bigger mystery was why she was standing a foot from his face, banging on the oak bed and as mad as a wet hen.

He sat up, grabbing the sheet as it slid off his naked body. Rosie might have bathed him as a boy, but he was self-conscious now. In fact, he was downright uncomfortable with her planted firmly in his bedroom, glaring at him as if he was poison.

"Who? What girl?" He struggled out of bed, the sheet still clutched around him, and bent over to snag his pants from the chair. He straightened with a yelp when Rosie smacked him on his rear with the kitchen utensil. It was like he was nine years old again.

"Don't play the innocent with me." She glared through narrowed eyes. "I want to know exactly what you did to poor little Miranda last night."

"I have no idea what you're talking about." He moved well out of range.

Eyes narrowed, Rosie stared a minute longer, then abruptly said, "I'll be waiting downstairs. You and I are having a talk, fella." She stopped halfway to the door and said, "And I'm still big enough to tan your britches, you understand?"

Blinking in bewilderment, Rik watched her go as he pulled on his jeans. He fished around for a clean t-shirt, finally settled for a slightly dirty one and headed downstairs barefoot. Rosie got upset from time to time, but he hadn't seen her this riled since he was a kid.

"Sit." Rosie greeted him brusquely as he entered the kitchen, her arms folded across her chest. "Talk."

"Coffee first." He headed for the coffee pot.

Rosie waved her spatula. "No coffee, no breakfast and no back talk, young man. Sit down."

Perplexed and puzzled, Rik sat. Maybe he'd woken up in a parallel universe, like in a sci-fi movie. Or maybe Rosie had been attacked by a rabid prairie dog and was undergoing a dramatic change of personality. If she started thrashing and foaming at the mouth, he was definitely calling the public health officer.

"Look at this." Rosie held up a note in feminine writing he recognized.

"Miranda stop by?" he asked, pretty sure he didn't want to know.

Rosie slammed the spatula on the table. "She left a note—a note! Said she couldn't come see me anymore." She slid the paper over to him. "Here. See for yourself."

"Thanks for everything you've done for me and everything you've tried to do," he read. "I'm going to miss your company, but I think it's best if I stay away from the ranch until I leave. Rik will explain. Give my love to Hazel. M."

Rosie snatched the note back and tucked in her pocket. "Explain already."

"I don't understand either." Confusion filled his face, and Rosie softened.

"Did the two of you have another fight?"

"Not really." Rik searched his memory of the night before. The ride from the diner to ranch had been accomplished in silence. When she'd pulled up at his front door, Miranda said, "I've got the census on your place done. I'll have Frank order a copy for you." She deftly ducked his attempted kiss as he said goodbye, but there was nothing new in that.

"Did you do something stupid?" Rosie fixed him with a stern look.

"No." That was true enough. He wasn't about to tell Rosie he'd come up with a Plan B, especially while she was in this mood. He'd probably get that spatula to the side of his head if he announced his new tack in wooing Miranda was to pretend he didn't care.

Rosie fired another question. "You didn't try anything out of line, did you?"

"Of course not!" Rik slumped back in his chair and buried his hands in his hair, exasperated. "We went to the meeting last night. We stopped for a sandwich on the way home. She told me the ranch count was almost over. She drove away. End of story."

Rosie sniffed, and Rik had the feeling she didn't believe him. Still, he wasn't concerned until she untied her apron, handed him the spatula and said, "Fix your own breakfast. I'm going to Hazel's." That quick she was gone, leaving Rik staring after her.

Rik was nowhere to be found by the time Rosie came roaring up to the house. She marched in, dropped her purse on the settee in the hall and went room to room, making certain he wasn't home. With a sigh of satisfaction, she headed back out to the kitchen and started rifling through cupboards and freezer. As she pulled out a thick package of steaks, she crossed her fingers and muttered a little prayer that Hazel's crazy plan would work. If it didn't, and Miranda refused to speak to that stubborn man again, the Hallowell ranch might end up in the hands of some anonymous business. Shoving away the thought, she decided chocolate cherry cheesecake was more romantic than the coconut pie she'd planned. And romance was the order of the day. Or, rather, night.

\*\*\*\*

The inside of Miranda's little cabin seemed more stifling than ever. If it hadn't been for the window air conditioning unit going full blast, she would have blamed the weather. If she'd had the sniffles, she might have chalked it up to a fever.

She had what her mother called "the blahs." She wasn't sick, exactly. She simply didn't feel like doing anything except lounging on the couch and staring out the window. She'd stayed in to finish the mountain of paperwork that had piled up, but gave up after she read the same lines over and over.

She sighed. Nothing made sense these days. She'd had such an orderly existence before coming to Colorado, planned perfectly and meticulously carried out. A growing rainy day fund, a savings account for a house down payment and a modest annual contribution to Brittani's college fund were her springboard to a perfect future.

Finding new determination, she stood, stretched and turned her attention back to her paperwork. Starting now, she was taking control of her life again. No ups and downs, no giddy emotions to hold her common sense hostage. She'd lived without Rik for ten years, and she would manage to live without him for the rest of her life. There was no place in her plan for that man.

She'd settled at the kitchen table with a stack of clean report forms and two newly-sharpened number two pencils, the kind Frank insisted were best, when she heard the honk of a car horn outside the cabin. Sighing, she walked to the front door, peeping out through its small glass window to check on her visitor. If it was Rik, she'd simply tell him he wasn't welcome here.

Instead she saw Hazel and Rosie picking their way over the gravel to the porch. Hazel carried a large wicker basket slung over one arm.

Miranda stepped onto the porch. "This is a surprise."

"We ought to be hanging our heads in shame," Rosie said.

"Yes, we realized you'd never received an official visit from the welcoming committee of the Armont Ladies Civic League, so we took it upon ourselves to come right away," Hazel said, patting the basket.

Miranda smiled. "I didn't know the civic league had a welcoming committee."

"It does now," Rosie muttered under her breath. She said, in a louder voice, "Oh, you'd be surprised what we have in Armont. Now let's get started."

Out the basket came an unusual array of things. There was a key chain from the Armont Branch of the Colorado State Bank—"You know, dear, that little trailer on the corner past the Cattleman's'—as well as a certificate for lunch at the diner, a free video rental from the grocery store, a scented candle from Viv's Beauty Boutique and Gift Shop, and a certificate that Hazel saved until last.

"This is something created for you, dear," she said, her head nodding as she spoke. Rosie's head bobbed in agreement like a bobble-head doll on a car dash. Caught up in that image, she missed part of what Hazel said, but caught the last part about a "welcome to Armont" picnic that very night at Hazel's second-oldest niece's father-in-law's cabin.

"Show up looking pretty," Rosie said. "You're the guest of honor, after all."

Hazel patted Miranda's hand. "This will be such a treat. You need to be at the cabin at 6 p.m. sharp. The driving directions are right there on the certificate."

"Oh, yes, dear," Rosie agreed. "Six p.m. sharp. Promise?"

"I promise." Miranda unconsciously crossed her heart. "Six o'clock."

Away from the cabin, the two women indulged in a bit of celebratory giddiness.

"I think that went quite well," Rosie said. "You were perfect as the welcome lady."

"And you managed not to give away a thing," Hazel complimented her. "Now if we can do as well with that stubborn boy…"

Finding Rik turned out to be harder. They spotted his truck easily enough at the edge of the high ridge, but Rik was nowhere to be found. Not to be deterred, the duo settled in on the grass behind the truck, splitting a single warm bottle of root beer that Rosie found in the car and a roll of hard candies from Hazel's purse. They finished their snack before they spied Rik coming toward them, a length of rope over his shoulder and a look of disgust on his face.

"Oh, dear, are you having a bad day?" Rosie struggled to her feet, ignoring the arthritic twinges in her knees, and greeted him. "You look awfully hot and tired."

"That's an understatement." He slung the rope into the truck bed and lifted out a tall insulated jug. He bent and turned on the spigot, letting the stream of water run into his mouth and over his face.

Hazel nudged Rosie, goading her into action.

"I suppose you wonder why we're out here," she said.

Rik wiped his face and stared at her with a smile. "The thought did cross my mind. I can't remember the last time I saw you out of the house at midday in this heat. And I do have my cell phone."

He closed his eyes and pinched his forehead, as if in deep thought.

"Wait, I'm getting an image...yes, it's clearer now. You won one of those magazine sweepstakes you're always entering and you've come up to tell me you want to take this ranch off my hands, so I can return to civilization."

Hazel giggled. Rosie frowned and said, "Oh, you're such a tease. You know perfectly well if I'd won a sweepstakes, I'd be on my way to Hawaii right now."

Rik laughed. "So what does bring you two ladies out here?"

"Things have been so muddled lately I forgot to tell you something very important," Rosie said.

"What might that be?"

She swallowed hard and fibbed. "The ladies league summer potluck is tonight and I promised you'd be the speaker."

"You what?" Rik stared at Rosie so hard she almost confessed her lie. But with a poke to the ribs from Hazel, she brazened it out.

"I told them you'd talk about investing in today's stock market," she said, compounding the lie. "They were thrilled to have such an important businessman as the keynote speaker."

"You didn't remember this at breakfast?" Rik's eyes darkened.

"At breakfast, you were all upset about Miranda."

"I was not," he snapped, so quickly Rosie knew he was still upset. "Besides, you've had plenty of other chances. When did you offer my services?"

"Yesterday," Hazel said quickly. "The speaker cancelled, and Rosie said you'd be glad to do it."

Rosie's head bobbed. "You will, right?"

Rik stared hard at the two women. When it came to negotiating, he'd rather face any CEO over a bargaining table than these two. No matter how much he argued, he was bound to lose. He sighed again and said, "Fine. When and where?"

"That cabin of Ralph Oxley's up above the ranch, the one he rents out for parties and tourists and such. He's Hazel's niece's father-in-law, you know, so we don't have to pay. Six o'clock sharp," Rosie said, trying to keep the glee from her voice.

"Dress nice," Hazel added. "Like a successful businessman."

They were giddy with excitement by the time they got back to the ranch. All they had to do was set things up at the cabin, and things should go off without a hitch.

Shortly before the appointed hour, Hazel nailed a big "Welcome" sign on the cabin, and Rosie put the finishing touches on a romantic dinner. The three-room cabin, a summer retreat before Ralph bought it, had been transformed. A white linen tablecloth covered one of the round tables, and an arrangement of roses and greenery, quickly put together by one of Hazel's many nieces, stood as a centerpiece. Rosie brought the best china and silver from the Hallowell collection, and as a final touch, added the footed silver ice bucket used only for Christmas and special occasions. Filled with ice, it held a bottle of champagne.

"I think we're ready." Hazel's hands flitted nervously across the cloth, smoothing out invisible wrinkles.

"Well, the food is." Rosie had everything in serving dishes over warmers: Steaks, two baked potatoes, Rik's favorite broccoli side dish, and the candied sweet potatoes Miranda had given her the recipe for. She took two crisp salads from the refrigerator and set them at the twin place settings before quickly penning a note that read "Cheesecake in the fridge." She slipped it under the ice bucket.

Hazel looked at her watch and said, "Five minutes. Take your place."

Rosie stationed herself outside the cabin, while Hazel hovered inside the door. The first vehicle to arrive was Rik's. Rosie dashed out to grab him as soon as he stepped foot from the vehicle.

"Where is everyone?" he frowned. "You did say six, right?"

"Oh, the speaker always comes early," she said blithely "Let's go in the back door. I want to hear your speech, and you can give it to me in the kitchen while the others are arriving."

She'd barely hustled him off when Miranda pulled up.

Hazel rushed out to greet her, smiling in approval at her appearance. Miranda was wearing a full-skirted dress that made the best of her figure, and she'd done her hair up into a sophisticated twist.

"Am I too early?" Miranda looked around her in puzzlement. "I thought you said it started at six."

"We thought you could help with the last-minute arrangements," Hazel said, steering her toward the cabin. "It's always nice to have another pair of hands."

She gestured toward the lot outside. "Is that Rik's truck?"

"Rosie's car started making a funny noise, so she borrowed it for the evening."

As soon as Rosie heard the front door open, she said hastily, "Oh, Rik, they're here." She shoved him through the kitchen door into the dining room, stammering, "You run along, and I'll be right there."

She hurried out the back door, turning the lock behind her as she stepped outside and pulled it shut. She walked briskly to the front of the cabin, where Hazel was at the door.

"Done!" Hazel mouthed, dangling a key from her fingers. Rosie gave her a thumbs up and headed for Hazel's sedan. She gave a big sigh as they started back down the road.

"Do you think it will work?"

Hazel nodded. "Ralph had new locks put on when he bought the place. One key opens both doors, and there are only two keys. I have one, and he has the other. The only way they're getting out of there tonight is if they dig a tunnel or bust down the door."

"What are you doing here?" Rik stopped short and stared at Miranda. "I'm supposed to be talking to the civic league."

"And I'm supposed to be enjoying a picnic welcoming me to the area."

"I can't believe they did this.

"I can." Miranda couldn't believe she'd fallen for the ruse. "What I can't believe is that we didn't see it coming."

"How could we?" Rik prowled around, looking for another way out. But short of breaking one of the narrow, high windows and shouting to help, he didn't see one.

He dropped down on a bench and spread his arms out behind him. "Well, here we are." He looked around him and spotted the elegantly-spread table. "At least they intended to feed us."

Miranda walked over and lifted the lids of the serving dishes. "Really well, too. Steak, baked potato, and the trimmings." She shrugged her shoulders. "Care to join me for dinner?"

"I'm starving." He grabbed a plate and speared a steak. "If you'd rather not eat with me, I can sit over there. I read your note this morning, and it seems I'm definitely *persona non grata.*"

"Tell you what, we'll call a truce." She forked the other steak onto her plate. "At least until they spring us. I'm too hungry to be mad." She motioned toward the table the women had prepared. "For our own safety, we need to share a table. By the looks of the other ones, cleaning is a haphazard occurrence."

Rik agreed warily, perplexed by the change in Miranda's mood. The note he'd seen this morning had prepared him for sheer and total hostility, but she was acting downright hospitable. Nice, even. Bordering on cordial.

That worried him nearly as much as being trapped in this place for who knew how long. Physically, he was stronger and, although Miranda was agile, he thought he could take her if worse came to worse. But mentally, she had the advantage. She was a woman, and that certainly had to help when two other females had laid a trap.

"You didn't have anything to do with this, did you?" he asked, his suspicions aroused.

"Good lord, no." Miranda stared at him in near-horror. "What in the world would possess you to think I'd volunteer to be locked up with you?"

"I know, I know, last man on earth, and all that," he said wearily. "Let's not damage my ego any more than it is, okay? There was a time when I thought I was a pretty swell guy, but apparently I was wrong. Not only will you not agree to marry me, now you can't even stay friends with Rosie because of my despicable presence."

Miranda wagged a forkful of lettuce at him. "We declared a truce, remember? We will eat civilly, like strangers who happen to be stranded together, but nothing more. Let's change the topic."

"Looks like the price of cattle might go up," Rik said resignedly, having learned cattle futures and the ripening of the grain on nearby spreads was about all they could discuss without wandering into a forbidden area of conversation. To his surprise, Miranda laughed and asked about Armont's history, giving him a chance to brag about the town that had housed Hallowells for four generations.

Halfway through his explanation as to how the women's civic league had been created to appease the wives who hated their husbands hanging around the Cattleman's Club, he realized he was thirsty. Incredibly thirsty. So thirsty he didn't think he could swallow again without a drink. He recalled that everything had seemed a little salty in the first few bites, and wondered if the women had found some other way to ruin his day.

He choked out, "I need a drink," and headed for the kitchen. Miranda's "Get me one, too!" ran in his ears.

A neatly lettered sign above the sink said, "Water must be boiled for safety. Owner". He checked the refrigerator and found no liquid there.

"Damn." He scrubbed a hand across his face. They'd left only one choice.

He walked back into the other room and waved toward the bottle

"It's this or nothing."

"You've got to be kidding." Miranda went out to the kitchen to check for herself. She grabbed a flute from the table on her return and said, "That ice is melting. Give me some of that water."

Rik frowned. "No way. Knowing those two, they've probably done something to it. It won't hurt us to drink a little bit of this." He popped the champagne cork and filled both glasses halfway. "Just enough to take care of the salt."

By the time the evening sun gave way to the dark of night, the cheesecake was gone and they'd run out of safe conversation topics. No one had come to rescue them and it looked like they might be stuck for a long, long time. Finally, deciding he might as well enjoy himself, Rik refilled his champagne glass.

"Here." He filled Miranda's as well. "Let's toast to something."

"Like what?"

"Old times. Conniving middle-aged women. Better times. Who cares?" He gestured with his glass, said "To us" and drank until the flute was empty. He reached for the bottle and filled his glass again.

"Hit me again." He half-filled the flute Miranda held toward him, and then shook the empty bottle.

"Looks like we're out. Unless you want me to open the warm bottle in the kitchen,"

Miranda shrugged. "I'm not picky."

Rik opened the bottle.

Her glass refilled, Miranda made a toast: "Here's to faithful friends and faithless men" while she tipped the glass at Rik. As the bubbling liquid slid down her throat, she couldn't decide which she enjoyed more, the look on Rik's face or the tickle of the champagne bubbles.

She drank a little more, then more. She held the flute toward Rik.

"One more time, big boy." She giggled.

"Your wish is my command." He filled her flute to the top, then his. She realized he was keeping up with her, glass for glass.

She also realized she wanted to kiss him, to loosen his shirt and run her hands up his back. She wanted to feel his lips on her naked flesh and taste his. She wanted to feel the contours of his body, feel how it differed from that of the boy she'd loved. She wanted Rik, right here and right now.

More than anything, she wanted to know if he was feeling that same urge…even if acting on that urge was the stupidest thing the world they could do.

Chapter Thirteen

Miranda found the radio at the same time Rik discovered the chocolate dipped strawberries in the refrigerator. A few minutes later, music poured through the room as Rik invited Miranda to dance.

The champagne dulled their memories. He no longer remembered he was playing hard to get; she forgot she was completely, absolutely through with this man. She stepped into the arms he offered, leaned against his hard body and laid her head upon his chest.

It was like going home. For the first time in weeks, she felt at ease with Rik as they moved slowly across the floor to the strains of a soft country song. She closed her eyes and let him guide her, her mind blank to all but this moment in time.

When the song ended, another ballad followed. The pause in their dancing was only momentary and the feeling as wonderful throughout the second tune. The slow fade-out of the music led to an announcer's smooth voice and Rik's hand capturing hers and leading her to the table that held the strawberries.

"Ooh, make me a goddess," Miranda sighed as she settled on the table. "I've always wanted a moment of total decadence."

She leaned back on her elbows and smiled at Rik, wiggling as she settled into place. Answering her smile with a wide grin, he picked a plump strawberry and brought it to her open lips. She bit off a juicy bite before snatching the berry to treat him with the second bite. Rik nudged closer and settled between her thighs as they feasted on the rest of the fruit, delicately licking a bit of juice that escaped from the corner of her mouth.

Deep inside, Miranda knew this was so, so wrong. She was avoiding Rik, not wrapping her arms around his neck as he bent down to kiss her. Sighing and returning that kiss, encouraging him to do more was the big no-no.

Which seemed more like a big yes-yes-yes as his lips moved from her mouth to the swell of her breasts and his hands tugged at the buttons that lined the front of her summer dress. She wiggled until it dropped to the floor, leaned forward so he could unfasten the clasp of her bra. At this moment her mind was muddled on a lot things, but one was crystal clear: She wasn't about to stop now.

The suit jacket and tie Rik had been wearing earlier had been tossed on a table somewhere between the opening of the first bottle of champagne and the end of it. That made things easier for Miranda as she squinted and undid his shirt buttons, one after another.

Her hands moved across his naked, muscled chest; its contours familiar and yet new. His breath, hot against her cheek, carried the sweet scent of the bubbly wine. Despite the callouses, his hands, caressing the small of her back as she undressed him, were gentle. She leaned into them as she pulled the shirt from his trousers, then ran down the zipper of his pants.

Soon they were naked. Almost. Miranda wore tiny silk panties; Rik wore only boxers that accentuated his need rather than hiding it.

"God, I've missed you." His words came out as a hiss when Miranda pressed against him, teasing him.

"Good." She rose to her toes and began to sway in time to the music still filling the room. "I've always dreamed of being unforgettable."

She wrapped her arms around his neck, entwined her fingers in his hair. She leaned into him, encased in the cage of his arms, the past forgotten and the future unimagined. This moment, this need was all that mattered.

"There's a better place for this," Rik whispered when the music ended. Slipping strong arms beneath her, he carried her to the small bedroom where a thick candle filled the room with the scent of roses.

"Damn, they thought of everything," Rik whispered. He placed her on the bed and facing her, lay down beside her and pulled her to him. This was what he'd longed for; what he'd wanted from the moment he'd seen her on that dusty road.

"You are so beautiful," he whispered, his hand tracing the round contours of her body. She nuzzled her head against him and his grip tightened. "And I want you so damn bad."

"Then take me." Her words were slightly slurred from the champagne.

"Not like this. Not when you're drunk and I'm close to it myself. When we make love, and we will, it's going to be at the time and place of our choosing, not because we're trapped together."

"This is a good enough time and place." Her words were faint.

"But not perfect." When her only reply was a sigh, Rik knew she'd be asleep in a moment. He held Miranda until her breathing changed and he knew she'd fallen asleep. He extricated himself from her hold with great care, folding the quilted coverlet over her after he slipped out of bed. He wandered into the great room and found there was a bit of champagne left in the bottle. Pouring it into a glass, he made a silent toast to the ingenuity of Rosie and Hazel. He didn't mind having a couple of helpers on his side, even though they came up with some of craziest plans he'd ever seen.

\*\*\*\*

Miranda woke to a splitting headache, full sunlight and a nearly naked Rik snoring beside her. She sat up in horror, regretting it as the pounding in her head reached the sensation of a full-size brass band playing a rousing Sousa march.

Clutching her temples, she eased out of bed. Her heart sank when she realized all she wore were panties.

What the hell had she done?

Moving as fast as her aching head would let her, she sneaked out of the room and went looking for her clothes. She scrambled into them, each piece another part of the armor she needed to resist Rik, not caring if the dress was wrinkled and smelled faintly like champagne. Standing still, she tried to remember exactly what had led to her being undressed and asleep with Rik.

Her mind refused to cooperate.

She found her purse and searched for the tiny bottle of non-aspirin pain reliever that should be somewhere in the bottom. Finding the container and grateful for its three-pill contents, she looked for something to take them with.

The reminder about boiling water kept her from using tap water. She checked the two champagne bottles and discovered just enough left in one to wash down the pills. She swallowed both with a grimace; flat champagne was not the right choice. Not at all.

She sat at the table and laid her head on her arms. She couldn't remember how long it took the stupid pills to kick in, but she had no intention of facing the day–or Rik–until her brain was back in functioning mode. She longed to try her mother's remedy for a headache, which consisted of a strong cup of coffee and a chocolate bar, but this place was sadly lacking in that sort of amenity.

Maybe if she stayed really, really still, her head would stop spinning. She closed her eyes with their heavy lids and adjusted her position. She'd rest for just a minute before confronting whatever sins she'd committed last night.

The sun had moved by the time Miranda woke with a start. She must have dozed off. Slowly raising her head, she realized the brass band had been reduced to very faint elevator music. She might just live after all.

Now it was time to figure out exactly what she'd done last night.

"Rik!" She shouted his name from the bedroom doorway, wincing only slightly. "Wake up. Now!"

His moan, followed by a curse, was oh, so satisfying. If she had to suffer, so did he.

"What happened last night?" she demanded.

"We both drank too much champagne, danced a little, took off our clothes and I carried you to bed."

Miranda gritted her teeth.

"After that? What happened after that?"

Under any other circumstances, Rik would have enjoyed her discomfort and toyed with her a little before confessing the truth. But he couldn't look at her pale face and troubled eyes and lie.

"Nothing you didn't want," he said. "The choice was yours. I distinctly hearing you ask me to take you." He paused before adding, "In a carnal way."

"I know what means," she snapped. "That doesn't make waking up naked next to you any easier."

"You weren't quite naked," he pointed out. "I, on the other hand, am. You're welcome to stand there and enjoy the view, but I feel it only fair to warn you. I'm tossing off these covers and standing up now."

Rik laughed as she grabbed the knob and slammed the door, putting a barrier between them. If she couldn't remember, she'd imagine what might have happened. He suspected that the longer she thought about it, the wilder those imaginings would become. He also wondered if she'd believe him when he told her they hadn't made love, that she'd gone to sleep instead.

Probably not.

"I'm coming out," he called, pulling on his briefs. He opened the door to discover she wasn't anywhere around. He yanked on his pants and padded barefoot through the small lodge.

Miranda was nowhere to be found.

On his second trip to the kitchen, he tried the back door. It opened easily. He headed to the front door and tried that one too, turning the handle to discover it had also been unlocked.

He hadn't heard a vehicle start up. Shoving his sockless feet into his shoes, he slung on his shirt as he headed outside. Miranda's car was still there; she was all that was missing.

"Miranda!" He shouted her name and waited for a reply.

Nothing. He called again, but to no avail.

He rounded the cabin intent on finding her. When he did, he stopped short, divided about whether to comfort her or slip away unseen. She was sitting on a rock at the back of the property, huddled into herself. Her face was buried in her crossed arms and he had a feeling she was crying.

Damn, he'd screwed up again. He should have set her mind at ease immediately. He should have stayed up all night instead of climbing in beside her. But in his champagne-dulled mind, sleeping with her had made perfect sense. What could it hurt if he held her for a time, dozed off with her in his arms, her body warm against his?

"Hey." He walked toward her, not sure of what his next move would or should be.

No answer. He dropped onto the ground next to her and tipped his head to study her damp eyes, all he could see of her face.

He was the world's biggest ass. He couldn't seem to stop hurting her.

"What do you want?" She turned her head to hide her face against her shoulder.

"To let you know nothing happened. Not that I didn't want it to. Trouble is, that champagne was speaking for you."

Miranda lifted her head.

"Why should I believe that?" she asked, her face wary.

"Because among my many flaws, there's still a kernel of gentlemanly behavior. I did make you a promise, though. There's going to be a time and place for us to do what we almost did last night. We're both going to be wide awake, sober and in complete agreement."

"Yeah. And pigs are going to be flying any time now."

She stood and started walking away, her steps steady and her back straight and proud. Rik watched her go, ready to tell her what was in his heart: That he loved her. That he wanted to get to know his daughter. That the family they'd make might fill the void he'd felt in his life for far, far too long. He followed her around the building, close enough to hear her loud "Damn!" and what sounded like a hard kick to her car. By the time he reached her, she had the hood up and was staring into the engine's innards.

"What did those scheming women do to my car?" she asked.

Rik moved to the front of the vehicle and looked everything over. Finally he saw several spark plug wires that had been pulled off the plugs. It was a simple way to disable a car and took only a minute to fix.

"Try it now," he said, slamming the hood back down.

The engine roared to life when Miranda turned the key. Rik stepped back and she drove past him without even a wave or a honk of the horn. Pissed, he headed for his own car wondering what those two women had done to his. To his surprise, it started right up. Narrowing his eyes against the morning sun, an action necessitated by the headache that was starting to build, he headed back to the ranch.

Rosie had better be there, and she'd better be ready to explain. He was an idiot to have fallen for her excuse of being sick. The woman was the picture of perfect health and besides, someone recuperating from whatever Rosie was supposed to have had could never concocted and carried out this quasi-kidnapping. He intended to take a hot shower and hit his own bed when he got back home, but not until Rosie had endured a little interrogation.

His thoughts got darker as he neared the ranch. Was his mother still trying to pull the strings long-distance? He wouldn't put it past her to promise Rosie a cash bonus if she managed to hook him up with a woman who would keep him in Colorado. Mom was nearly as bad as Rosie in managing to get her way, but he wasn't about to let either of them run his life. He was doing just fine screwing it up by himself.

****

Miranda cruised through what passed as a downtown in Armont, being careful not to attract the attention of the town's one and only lawman. The last thing she needed was to get a ticket in a government car. Frank would learn about the ticket and with her luck, he'd also learn that she was hung over when she got it.

As she passed the Cattleman's, she saw Junie walking out. Hitting the brakes, she swerved into the lot and stopped beside the other woman. She rolled down the window and leaned out.

"You win," she said. "Rik Hallowell is all yours."

She shot back out of the lot before Junie could respond. There. One detail was taken care of. Rik wouldn't have time to bother her with Junie hot on his heels.

Miranda tried to put Rik from her mind as she made the drive to her cabin. She focused on the next day's work, the monthly report due to Frank on Tuesday and making a mental shopping list of what Brittani would need for school in a few weeks. But Rik's words kept distracting her.

*"I did make you a promise, though. There's going to be a time and place for us to do what we almost did last night. We're both going to be wide awake, sober and in complete agreement."*

Chapter Fourteen

Rosie was wisely absent when Rik rolled into the house. A note stuck on the refrigerator with an apple magnet informed him she'd gone shopping and other errands and wouldn't be back until mid-afternoon. He toyed with calling Miranda, insisting she listen to him, but wound up tossing the phone on the pillow-laden couch. The way she'd roared away made it pretty clear that she'd meant it when she said she wanted to be left alone.

Well, he had news for her. He wasn't going to give up being a father that easily. Either she sat down with him and hashed it out or her lawyer would be sitting down with his.

Anger and determination colored his thoughts. By the time he finished his shower, he'd made up his mind. So she didn't want to see him. Fine. He'd put some distance between them so she wouldn't have worry about it.

A half-hour later, he stuck his own note on top of Rosie's. It simply read, "Be gone a day or two." He was a grown man and didn't have to answer to a housekeeper or, by extension, his mother. He needed time away from this place, away from all the things that didn't fit with the life he'd planned for himself and his future.

His stomach growled as he rolled through the ranch gates; he headed for the Cattleman's instead of the airport. The vague physical effects of last night's booze would turn into something worse if he didn't get something in his stomach.

To Rik's relief, the parking lot was nearly empty. The breakfast regulars had been and gone and it was a little early for the lunch bunch. He walked in, picked a booth as far from the door as possible and sprawled across the seat. Fifteen minutes later, a massive cheeseburger and pile of fries sat before him.

He made quick work of both and was getting up to pay when the door opened and Junie walked in.

She was damn hot, he decided as she spotted him and started his way. Too bad her personality didn't match the package.

"Hey," she said in greeting. "You look like you had a rough night."

"I was up late with a situation," he said. "A little sleep and I'll be fine."

Junie tipped her head and smiled.

"My place is right down the road and I have one of those fancy foam mattresses," she said. "You're welcome to take a nap there anytime."

Rik managed to suppress a shudder. Within hours, everyone in Armont would know his car had been parked in front of Junie's house in broad daylight. By tomorrow, Rosie and her circle would be plotting to make that a permanent, till death do us part thing.

"Can't," he said. "I'm flying out this afternoon on business."

Junie brushed her lacquered fingertips down his chest. "Let me know when you're coming back and I'll make you a welcome-home dinner. We can make a special evening of it."

Rik stepped back and forced a smile.

"My plans are really uncertain. Thanks anyway."

He walked around her and on to the cash register. The last place he intended to ever be was at Junie's house, and he certainly had no plan to discover what she considered a special evening to be.

Heading toward Nevada, Rik looked down at the world beneath him from the cockpit of his plane and wondered how his life had gotten so crazy. He should be interviewing candidates for ranch manager now instead of heading to Vegas to see his brother. Knowing Ron would be shocked to see him walk up to whatever mansion he'd traded his inheritance for gave Rik a grim satisfaction. Why shouldn't his brother suffer a little, too?

If Miranda wanted him to stay away, he would. The worst of the problems at the ranch had been fixed, and he'd created a computer program to handle the financials. He was done doing penance. Staying there to satisfy his father's demands had kept him from meeting Miranda on schedule. That led to a daughter whose life he had missed and was still missing. He'd been punished enough.

****

"Nice place," Rik muttered to himself as he stopped the rental car in front of Ron's house. The Spanish-style structure was raw in its newness, the lawn still brown and lacking landscaping. So this was what their father had worked for all his life, a cookie-cutter mini-mansion in a town that had been built on other people's vices.

Instead of pushing the ornately-framed doorbell, Rik banged on the front door with a heavy hand. He took satisfaction in the expressions that flitted across his brother's face when he saw him–recognition, concern, fear and finally a wariness that settled in his eyes.

"Stopping by on your way back home?" Ron asked as he motioned Rik to come in.

"Nope. This is a special visit just to see you." He moved into a spacious formal living room without waiting for an invitation and sat in a wing chair.

"Can I get you a drink?"

Rik shook his head. "I'm not planning on staying long."

"Well, I need one." Ron went to the far side of the room and stepped behind a mirrored partition. He returned with a glass of amber liquid and clinking ice cubes and sat on the sofa across from Rik. "Come to town for a show or you gonna hit the casinos?"

"Just to see my one and only bro." Rik settled back in the chair and brought one booted foot to rest on the opposite knee. "I've got an offer for you."

Ron nodded and took a long swig of his drink.

"If you'll go back and pretend to run the farm, I'll sell my half to you for a dollar. Hire someone competent to ride the fences and handle the cattle. Send the financials to me and I'll take care of all that. All I'm asking is that you live there and fill in the gaps."

The glass in Ron's shook so violently that Rik could hear the ice cubes clanging against each other.

"Hell, no," he finally said after he drained the glass. "That's why Dad left me money, because the ranch was yours."

"And I'm willing to sell it to you. Price too high? I'll drop it to a quarter."

"Traci would never leave this house."

"She will if the money's right. All the profits would be an even split between you and Mom. She'll understand."

"Damn you, Rik, I can't go back there." Ron leaned forward, pleading with his brother. "I was the screw-up, the son he regretted having. You could do wrong. Me, I couldn't do anything right. Every time I'd mess something up, he'd shout at me to go back in the house and play dolls like a sissy boy, that I would never be man enough to fill his boots.

"He told me I didn't know a bull from a heifer, that he was sick and tired of redoing everything I did. You want to know how often he swore and asked me why I couldn't be more like you? Every day, Rik. Every damn day."

Stunned, Rik stared at his brother and the tears that threatened to spill from Ron's eyes. All these years, he'd thought Ron wanted to stay in the house, close to their mother. Those times he'd bitterly fumed about the work dumped on him while Ron got off easy weren't what they seemed to be. He and his dad might have struck sparks sometime, but Rik had always known his dad had confidence in him. Apparently, all Ron had gotten was derision.

"I understand…now," he said, his voice a bit uneven. Because he finally did. He glanced around the spacious room and then rested his eyes on his brother. "This is a beautiful house and you're lucky to have Traci. Enjoy your new life."

Standing up to leave he did something he hadn't planned on, an act he hadn't performed for years. He hugged Ron, brother to brother, filled with the dawning realization that they weren't so different after all.

"Before long all we'll have is each other," he said, stepping back. "Losing Dad was tough; losing Mom's going to be harder, even if it's twenty years from now. We can't get back the time we lost but we don't have to waste any more. Soon as my life settles down, let's take a golf trip or go fishing, just us brothers. Deal?"

A big smile split Ron's face.

"Deal," he said. "I'd like that."

****

The mid-afternoon sun was striking the porch supports when Miranda woke up. Her headache had subsided to an occasional dull throb. She wasn't sure whether the relief came from sleeping in her own bed, taking even more pain killer or the combination of coffee and chocolate she'd consumed as soon as she reached home. She owed a huge debt of gratitude to whatever took her from a vise on her head to near-normalcy.

Pouring herself a glass of sweetened ice tea, she sat down cross-legged on the couch with her laptop and logged into her e-mail account. Her spirits lifted when she opened an attachment to find a picture of her mother with Brittani on the porch of her parents' home. Her mom looked great, considering what she'd just gone through, and Brittani's eyes sparkled–eyes that were nearly as blue as her father's.

Miranda closed the photo, guilt rushing through her. She'd had this wonderful child for nearly a decade, had experienced every important moment in her life. She'd denied Rik that opportunity. Not because he'd proved himself to be less than she'd thought or because she hadn't seen him as father material. She'd been too young to realize that plans and dreams could dissipate like dew, that the sharp edge of reality could cut away golden fantasies.

"What have I done?" she muttered, remembering the way Rik had held back at the airport, allowing her to maintain the pretense that he was nothing to her. Nothing to Brittani.

Shutting down her computer, she set the laptop on the couch and reached for her purse. She was going to the ranch. She was going to have that talk with Rik that should have taken place long ago. At the time she'd meant it when she said she didn't want to see him again, yet she knew that was impossible. Her daughter–their daughter–deserved two parents like all her friends.

As she bumped down the road, she practiced what to say. Dare she express affection for him without Rik trying to make more of it? Could she persuade him not to ask much of their daughter but give Brittani time to decide how she felt about having a father in her life, let alone one so far away?

Her stomach churned as she drove through the now-familiar gates. The house looked so imposing as she pulled closer and the Hallowell spread was huge. If Rik insisted on custodial visits, would Brittani be disappointed when she came back to Michigan? Here she could have all the pets she wanted, even a horse. Rosie had made it plain that Rik's mother wanted grandchildren, and he could present one already half-grown.

Taking a deep breath, she stepped out of the car and headed up the front steps. She rang the doorbell, expecting Rosie to answer.

Nothing.

She tried again with a similar lack of response.

Finally, she opened the door, stepped into the house and called first for Rosie and then Rik. Only silence answered her.

Disappointment flooded through Miranda as she walked slowly back to her car and headed the way she'd come. When the drive ended at the road, she turned toward Armont. Slowing as she came to the Cattleman's, she told herself she wasn't looking for Rik. She was hungry.

A different kind of loneliness than she'd experienced before sneaked in as she sat alone in the nearly-empty restaurant and ate a barbecue sandwich that deserved more appreciation than she was giving it. She was used to being alone, both while she was working and in her personal life. It came with the territory and suited her personality. Today, though, she felt invisible. No one stopped and spoke; even the waitress was busy at the other side of the room.

She was at the proverbial cross in the road, where whatever decision she made now would color the rest of her life. She wished she had that really good friend to talk to, someone who could act not only as a sounding board but an advisor. Her friends, though, were acquaintances, people she saw at Brittani's school activities or neighbors who said hello.

Finished nibbling at the sandwich, Miranda dropped a tip on the table and paid her bill at the front counter. She fumbled in her purse for sunglasses as she walked out into the sunlight. When a voice called her name, she jumped.

"How'd things go last night?"

She looked up to see Rosie's friend Hazel walking toward her.

"I'm not sure what Rosie expected, but it didn't happen," she said. "Rik's going his way and I'm going mine. I hope you're not too disappointed that all your work was in vain."

"Oh, honey, I'm sorry." Hazel gave her arm a sympathetic squeeze. "The two of you seemed perfect for each other. And I swear, the way he looked at you sometimes…"

Uncertain what to say to that, Miranda chose to remain silent. Hazel took the hint and changed the subject to the weather. After a short and stilted conversation about the likelihood of rain, Miranda finally got away.

She fought the impulse to go back to the ranch to see if Rik had returned. Maybe her father was right. Perhaps she ought to go back to Michigan, hire a good attorney and let the lawyers battle it out.

*And run away again.*

Rik's accusation still niggled at her. She hadn't run away from him, not at all. He failed to keep his promise, didn't show up and when she realized their child was growing inside her, she'd needed security and stability, two things her parents could give her in spades.

"To hell with it." The words echoed in the car. No way could she make a decision while she was here, in Rik's territory. Back home, with Brittani every day, she'd be able to think better.

At least she hoped she could.

\*\*\*\*

Ron's revelation stayed with Rik as he checked into a hotel on the Strip. He'd known their father could be an SOB sometimes, but to treat his own child in such a brutal, condescending way was unfathomable. He wondered how their lives would have been if Dad had been patient and taught Ron to the do the same things he'd taught Rik. Until now, Rik had always taken his father's tutelage for granted. He'd learned to string fences and brand cattle, to work on engines and the basics of both electricity and plumbing.

While he was becoming what his father called a "man's man," Ron had been banned from that world. He'd been dismissed as not worth the effort, with the expectation that he'd continue to fail.

Taking the elevator down to the casino floor, Rik resolved to forget the drama of the last few days. Tomorrow would be soon enough to pick up the reins at the ranch and resolve things with Miranda. Tonight was for fun.

He went through the motions until early morning, dropping money into the slot machines and at the gaming tables. He flirted with the pretty women serving drinks and struck up conversations with Midwesterners on vacation in Vegas. But his worries and regrets were still there as he called it a night and headed up to his room. If he was flying back in the afternoon, he needed to get some sleep.

Exhaustion and the drinks he'd had let him fall off as soon as he pulled the blankets up. He woke to the sleepy confusion of being in the wrong bed in an unremembered place; it took him a minute to realize he was in a Las Vegas hotel. A call to room service had breakfast on the way, and he grabbed a shower before the food arrived at his door.

He used his eating time to catch up on e-mails and messages concerning Domino and resisted the temptation to call both Miranda and Rosie. His talk with Miranda should be in person. He wanted to watch her expressive face and decide for himself what his chances were.

It would be too easy to fire Rosie long-distance–not that a firing would stick. His mother had hired Rosie, and he knew Mom would never agree to let her go. For all he knew, the housekeeper was getting a bonus for her little stunt.

Rosie, his mother and the alluring idea of a family were all on his mind as he flew back to Armont. The cracks in his perfect life were widening, letting him see the futility of going on as he had been. Money was great; so was respect for his business acumen. Yet moving up at Domino didn't seem as important now as it had two months ago when he'd returned to the ranch. Reputations faded, fortunes disappeared, but the kind of love a man felt for his woman and child–and their love for him–endured.

His temptation when he touched down was to call Miranda and demand that she listen to him. Common sense told him what a bad idea that was. The woman who'd ordered him to stay away wasn't likely to take a phone call. And since she was alone, a surprise visit to her cabin might get him shot, if she kept any kind of firearm for protection.

Rik stopped at the combination florist and dress shop that stood on the corner across from the Cattleman's. He walked in and ordered roses to be delivered to Miranda, signing the card himself.

*I'm a fool. R.*

He studied the message before handing the card back to the clerk. Maybe he should add "I'm sorry." Or "forgive me." Maybe he should cancel the order altogether, get the hell back to San Francisco and run the ranch long-distance.

"Sir?" The clerk was waiting with an envelope.

"Sorry." He handed her the card without making a change. "Will these still go out today?"

The clerk glanced at the clock. "It's a simple arrangement. That shouldn't be a problem."

He paid and headed out the door. Chances were Miranda would shred the flowers and toss them in the wind. Then again, she might decide to hightail to the ranch and give him what for. He'd take whatever she dished out for the opportunity to talk to her one more time, to plead his case, if not for love, at least for friendship.

## Chapter Fifteen

Miranda wiped the grit off her clothes and the dust from her face. She hadn't realized the wind was picking up until she was a half-mile from her car. Sunglasses had protected her eyes from the worst of the dirt and debris blowing around her, but the rest of her was in desperate need of a shower now that she was finally home. She grabbed her backpack and purse from the car and started toward the house. The sound of a vehicle approaching stopped her before she reached the porch.

She tensed, not wanting to turn around. She wasn't in a mood for visitors, especially the big three that seemed intent on making her otherwise-placid life into high drama–Rik, Rosie and Frank. Filled with reluctance, she turned to see an unfamiliar white van behind her car. She watched as a middle-aged woman got out with a wave, opened the back door of the van and started toward her with a crystal vase.

"I bet it's your birthday," the woman said as she headed toward Miranda. "He wanted to make sure these were delivered today." She chuckled. "You'd be surprised how many afternoon orders we get from boyfriends and husbands."

Miranda smiled and accepted the flowers with a simple "Thanks." Only one man would send her flowers, especially ones that were said to be the flower of love. These were beautiful, blood-red with velvety petals. She touched a stem; their thorns were still there. The roses were much like their relationship: sometimes lovely, yet capable of causing pain.

She carried them into the cabin and set them on the kitchen table where they brightened the weary area. It had been years since anyone had sent her flowers and she intended to enjoy them, even if they were from Rik. She pulled the card from inside the arrangement and read his note.

Those words stayed with her as she showered away the stress and dirt of the day, as she prepared a simple meal and ate it at the table where the flowers held center stage.

"I'm a fool."

What did he mean? Did he regret his casual assumption when they'd met again that she'd be up for another summer fling? Was he sorry he hadn't taken advantage of her in the cabin when she was willing to make love to him? Or had he taken some other action that he now regretted?

A cold feeling seized her. There had been ample time since their imprisonment for him to call an attorney and start the process of demanding visitation and custody. Men like Rik didn't have to wait weeks for appointments with lawyers. They kept them on retainer.

Miranda shoved her plate away. Her appetite was gone. Grabbing her purse and keys, she headed outside. She was about to break her own resolve to stay away; she had to know what he'd done.

****

Rosie watched the familiar sedan roll through the gates and toward the house. She hurried through the back door with the last bag of groceries, fully intending to stay in the kitchen until whatever was about to happen was over. She already knew things hadn't gone too well during what was supposed to be a romantic episode for Rik and Miranda. Hazel had sent her a text message warning her that their plan hadn't worked.

Hands busy putting away the refrigerator items, she listened to the ring of the doorbell and Rik's heavy steps as he came down from the second floor. She strained to make out their words after the front door opened and closed. When their voices grew louder, she regretted having made such quick work of the shopping.

"Rosie!" Rik's boomed from the adjacent room. "We'd like to speak to you."

She took a deep breath and let it out slowly. Her husband teased that she had a silver tongue and could talk her way out of anything. Oh, she hoped he was right.

"Coming!" she called back, frantically thinking up a defense as she slowly made her way to them. She had to make them understand how perfect they were for each other, even if they were too blind and stubborn to recognize it for themselves.

Rosie braced herself for anger when she finally joined them. Instead both faces were solemn.

"I know my mother wants you to find a way for me to come back here permanently," Rik said. "I'm sure she told you to use any means possible. However, I suspect trapping the two of us together with the intent of us getting drunk wasn't what she had in mind."

Before Rosie could defend herself, Miranda spoke up.

"Let's forget about the other night. I told Rik then what I'm telling you now: As soon as this assignment ends, I'm gone. Until then, no finding a way to throw us together. No invitations to dinner, no coaxing me to let Rik escort me somewhere–nothing. Got it?"

Rosie nodded. She wasn't sure she could speak around the lump in her throat. These two were perfect for each other, but they'd never admit it now. Rik had a streak of pride a Texas mile long and just as Hazel had predicted, Miranda was definitely an independent woman who didn't take well to being led. Tears prickled her eyes. She'd been picturing the children these two would have, beautiful ones with his eyes and her perfect features.

"As long as we have it straight," Rik said. She took his words for dismissal and walked rapidly back to her private domain. There in the kitchen, she gave vent to her emotions, wondering what was going to happen to this place now and whether she'd ever have the same relationship with Rik again.

****

"That went...well enough," Miranda said, fumbling for the right words.

"Rosie's feelings are hurt, but they shouldn't be." Rik blew out a frustrated breath. "Why the hell she thought she could play fast and loose with our lives, I don't know. I hope your boss doesn't find out we got drunk and spent the night together."

"The only way he can possibly find out is if someone tells. I have no intention of doing so, and I'm sure you don't either. I can't see Rosie giving him a call."

They were at the awkward moment where Miranda should be saying goodbye. She'd thanked him for the flowers; he apologized for letting things get as far as they did. There shouldn't be anything left to say.

Rik spoke anyway.

"Got a few minutes?"

"Maybe."

"I want to show you something."

She tipped her head and smiled slightly. "I've heard that line before."

Rik laughed. "Seriously, there's a place I want you to see before you leave. If I don't take you now, I may never have the opportunity."

Despite her misgivings, Miranda agreed. The look in Rik's eyes persuaded her. He seemed different today, not his usual flirting self.

"Can you ride a four-wheeler?" he asked.

She nodded.

"Good."

**** 

Their destination was a flat grassy plateau where a log house sat, roses growing around its posted porch. The grass was neatly mown and the flowerbeds along the walk were weeded.

"Who lives here?" Miranda asked.

"No one."

"But it's beautiful."

"When I was starting high school, Mom and Dad had a rough patch in their marriage. I was too young to understand that in marrying my father, my mother had given up more than she expected. She grew up with Virginia's lush rolling hills and ocean beaches. Colorado is different, both its terrain and its people.

"Dad was afraid he'd lose her and he did the only sentimental thing I'd ever seen from him. Without her knowing, he and a few friends built the house. He had grass seed and flowers shipped in from the East and he tried to create a little bit of home for her here."

He strode a few feet away and focused on the horizon. Miranda made her way down the path and stepped up onto the porch. A breeze cut through the summer heat, bringing the scent of roses with it. She leaned against a post, watching Rik and wondering what his teen years were like. She'd never doubted that her parents loved and wanted only the best for her. She suspected Rik hadn't felt the same acceptance and reassurance.

Brittani would be a teen in a few years, changing from being her mother's little girl to an independent woman of her own. Miranda intended for her to have the same loving support that she'd had. Could she do it by herself?

Her gaze slid toward Rik. His head was bowed; his sunglasses were held loosely between two fingers. In his stance she saw another similarity to her daughter.

"Rik!"

He turned, his expression neutral. Miranda realized as she walked toward him that the confidence he radiated was a protective shield that she'd managed to penetrate once. This might be an opportunity to have a real conversation with the man hidden behind the facade.

"About Brittani," she said.

His face tightened. "I told you I'd keep the secret until you decide it's the right time. You have my word. When you get ready to tell her, I'd like to be there."

"Of course!"

Rik's features softened. "I hate what's happened between us. For a while there, we were pretty good friends."

"We can still be," Miranda said hopefully.

"No." Rik shook his head. "Either we're less than that, two people connected by a child, or more."

"Like lovers." Miranda's words slid out on a whisper.

"Like two people who love each other," Rik corrected. "Husband and wife."

"Don't." Miranda's denial came on a shaky breath. "I need time. Being here, seeing you, it's too much."

"I'm not pushing you. I just want you to remember my offer still stands."

Miranda walked to her four-wheeler, unable to respond. Unwilling to respond.

Rik climbed on his own vehicle next to her and fired it up. They rode back to the ranch side by side, not speaking. Once there, Miranda stepped off and said a quiet goodbye. They'd said all they needed to; she was worn from the whirling thoughts that made her yearn for Rik at one moment and cautioned her to keep her distance the next.

# Chapter Sixteen

Miranda adjusted her seat upright and checked her safety belt as the flight attendant announced they were preparing to land in Detroit. In a few minutes, she'd walk into the airport where her parents and Brittani would be waiting. In two weeks, after her between-assignments vacation was over, she'd start in on the fruit of her animal-counting labors, compiling the data. She'd thought distance would help clear her mind and forget those moments of Rik's vulnerability. Instead, she remembered his face up at this mother's cabin and the tenderness in his eyes when he'd told her goodbye.

She didn't want to feel this way. She wanted to bundle up the last few weeks and put them in the place where she'd hidden her memories from 10 years ago. But like a caged bird, once free those memories couldn't be trapped again.

The plane touched down with the slightest of bumps. Miranda was one of the last to deplane. She returned the pilot's murmured goodbye as she headed toward her family and her future.

"Mom!" Brittani ran up and hugged her. "I didn't think you were ever getting off."

"I sat in the back. All those people had to get off before I could."

"Guess what, Mom?"

Miranda asked the expected "What?"

"I got my very first pet ever!"

Miranda's eyes widened. There was a strict policy at the apartment complex that banned all but service dogs. It looked like the first thing she had to do was break her daughter's heart and then have a long talk with her parents.

"Hey, kiddo, it's just a fish," her father said. "We had a long talk and Brittani knows that if she proves she can care of a fish, she might get a dog or cat later on."

*A fish. Yeah, they could handle a fish.*

"Mom, we gotta get your stuff." Brittani started tugging her down the corridor before she could give either parent a hug. With a rueful smile, Miranda fell in step with her daughter to be regaled with all the pent-up stories of a nine-year-old.

To Brittani's delight, she was allowed to pick out the restaurant for a welcome home dinner. Miranda was grateful when she picked a pizza place instead of fast food. After the guilty pleasure of the Cattleman's burgers, she had to ease herself back into the world of a meal in a bag.

Chattering through their midday meal and the two hour trip that followed, Brittani relived all things she'd done while her mother was gone. Even though Miranda knew about them from video chats and e-mails, she enjoyed the vivacious retelling.

"Tired, sweetie?" her mother asked Miranda from the front seat when she could finally break into Brittani's monologue.

"A little."

"Then why don't you two stay with us tonight instead of going on to your place? I've got a ham in the oven."

Miranda didn't want to stay, despite the bribe of her mother's honey-glazed ham. She wanted to be back in her own space and close out all the turmoil of the past weeks. But she couldn't bear to see disappointment replace anticipation on her mother's face after all her parents had done for her this summer.

"Sure. But don't expect me to be a social butterfly. I intend to conk out early."

By the time the supper dishes were done and Brittani was in bed, the fatigue that had ridden with Miranda on the plane was gone. She sat down with her parents to watch a TV police drama, but she had trouble getting into it. Her parents' cozy living room was a far cry from the cabin where she'd watched DVDs on that little player.

And Michigan was a far distance from Colorado, where she'd left part of her heart. She'd done the right thing. The only place for Rik in her life was as Brittani's other parent. She hated the idea of sending her daughter so far away on custodial visits, but Brittani would love the idea of a private plane with her father at the controls.

"What's wrong, honey?"

Miranda started at her mother's question.

"Nothing. Just watching the show."

"Oh. Do you think the junkie killed that guy or the lawyer?"

"Lawyer," Miranda said. "Junkie is too predictable."

"Since the chef at the fancy restaurant was the killer, I think you've got your mind elsewhere." Her father clicked off the television. "Would it help to talk about it?"

The voice in her head screamed No! But the words that came from her mouth were "We have to do it sometime, I guess."

Sadness flitted across her mother's features, and Miranda knew her dad had told the whole story. At least they weren't going to excavate the bones of her reckless relationship with Rik. She laid out the plans she'd made.

"I intend to invite him for Thanksgiving," she said, looking from one parent to the other. "If you're uncomfortable with Rik being here, we'll take Brittani and go to a restaurant instead of the family dinner. I think it will be easier for her to understand if they spend time together before we drop the bomb on her."

"So you want him to come here." Her dad's voice held a thoughtful note.

She nodded. "I plan to e-mail him tonight."

"You should ask him for a visit earlier." Her mother this time, sounding determined. "Dad and I have discussed it, and we don't see any reason to put it off."

Miranda felt a bubble of panic. She needed those weeks to decompress, to separate the emotional ups and downs of the summer from her plans for the future. She wanted Rik to have time, too. His determination to marry her might fade once he returned to his own life, too. She didn't want him to say or do anything in front of Brittani that might give her false hope. "Every child needs to know where they came from," her mother continued. "You owe it to Brittani to fill in the other half of who she is. The older she is before she learns about her father, the greater chance that she'll resent you for keeping her in the dark."

The subtle warning wasn't lost on Miranda. She had no intention of hashing things out tonight. Well-meaning as her parents were, this was her life and her decision.

"Can we talk about this later?" she asked. "I'm exhausted. All I want is a bath and bed."

"Of course, darling." Her mother rose. "I'll make sure there are towels in the upstairs bathroom."

When Miranda rose to follow, her father stopped her.

"Most times, the easy thing isn't the right thing," he said. "But you already know that, don't you?"

His words haunted her as she soaked in a tub of bubbles and then climbed into the double bed that had been hers since she was twelve. Down the hall was a little girl whose friends had fathers, whose families included more than a mother and a fish. Thousands of miles away was a man eager to truly be a father. She was the barrier between them, a wall that she knew Rik would scale if she didn't open the gate and let him in.

The solution was no clearer by the light of day. An emotional goodbye followed breakfast as Brittani prepared to leave her summer home. She settled down in the seat beside Miranda for the hour-long drive to their own place, popping in ear buds and turning on her MP3 player. With communication effectively cut off, Miranda was free to start worrying again.

By the time she reached their small town, her resolve was firm. She'd invited Rik for Thanksgiving; guilt wasn't going to make her change her mind. She and Brittani needed time alone to reconnect. School started in a week, and she wanted a little fun time for the two of them first.

"Brit!" she called loud enough to be heard through her daughter's music.

"Huh?"

"Pull the plug." She wasn't going to compete with the teeny-bop songs Brittani favored. A huge sigh accompanied Brittani's action was she shut off the music and took the ear buds out.

"Feel like school shopping tomorrow?" Miranda asked.

Her daughter's eyes lit up. "At the big mall?"

Miranda nodded.

"Can we get those shoes I told you about?"

"Maybe." Miranda wasn't sure her budget could include one hundred dollar shoes, but maybe they'd find them on sale. Or an imitation that would be just as good, "You make a list tonight and we'll leave right after breakfast."

"You are so cool," Brittani said, leaning over to hug her mother's arm. "Like the very coolest mom in the whole world."

Happiness bubbled in Miranda as Brittani put the earplugs back in and started her music again. She knew her daughter would probably change her mind when she was a little older, but Miranda intended to enjoy being the world's best mom for as long as she could.

****

"Thanks for stepping in, Bret."

"No problem, man," his friend murmured. "You'd do the same for me."

Rik would. Now. At the beginning of summer, things might have been different. He'd told Miranda then that he'd changed, he was a different man. Truth was, he was just now becoming a better Rik.

His brother's revelation had changed the way Rik saw both the past and the future. He hadn't argued with his father when his younger self was ordered to work off his debt. He hadn't even considered that there was no debt. He and Ron ate the same food, slept in the same house, got the same amount of allowance every week. Their father had kept Ron where he wanted him through intimidation and kept Rik on the ranch with guilt.

"I shouldn't be gone more than a few days. This thing back in San Francisco will work itself out soon, I hope."

Bret held up his hands in a stop motion. "We were, what, twelve or so when we cut our fingers and became blood brothers. You took the heat when I knocked that ball through my dad's window 'cause you knew I was pushing my luck. I'm finally getting around to returning the favor."

Rik had known Bret his whole life. Their parents were friends and, with so much distance between ranches, they'd become natural playmates. When they were old enough to drive, they doubled-dated and went to other, bigger places that offered more than Armont. In the end, though, Bret had chosen to stay a rancher and Rik had joined the army.

Their friendship had been renewed this summer. Bret was as solid as a friend could be, and Rik trusted him with the important job of rounding up cattle for sale.

Eventually, he'd hire a manager. With Bret's help, he could put that off until after his mother came home and they had a long talk about her expectations. It was a talk they should have had when his father died. Instead, Rik had arrived just in time for the funeral and left the next day. Ron's disappearance was the only thing dramatic enough to bring him back.

Leaving his plane behind, he took a commercial flight to San Francisco so he could work on the plane. A project months in the works looked like it might fall apart, and he needed to be at Domino until things got straightened out.

His office was just as he left it, down to the paper clip next to his keyboard. Although it had obviously been cleaned, care had been taken not to disturb anything. He winced at the memory of how he'd bite someone's head off if things weren't exactly as he wanted them.

His apartment, when he got to it late that night, was cold and sterile after the ranch house. He'd picked out the black leather sofas and glass-and-chrome tables himself. He'd had the walls painted white and refused to let his mother enhance the decor the first time she came to visit. This wasn't a home. It was a stopping place.

He wanted desperately to call Miranda. He needed to hear her voice, to know that she'd gotten home safely. But they'd made an agreement. No contact until Thanksgiving when he'd travel to Michigan and officially meet his daughter.

*His daughter*. The reality of fatherhood filled him with anticipation. Did she have Miranda's open acceptance of new people and places, or was she shy with strangers? Was she one of the brightest kids in the class or did she struggle with history the way he had? What was her favorite color, her favorite movie, her favorite toy?

Damn. He'd missed so much. He understood why Miranda thought he'd forgotten about her. Chance meeting, instant attraction, nights of hot sex…definitely the elements of a summer fling.

Guilt flooded him. While he'd been busy resenting his father and building a life that didn't involve Colorado and ranching, Miranda had been barely scraping by as she made a home for his child. *To hell with it*. He was calling her.

Every call he made to her cell phone went straight to voice mail. He gave up after the fourth one. Of course she wasn't answering. Wait until Thanksgiving, she'd asked and he agreed. Labor Day had come and gone, September had faded into October and his reunion with Miranda and his daughter was only six weeks away.

Sighing, he popped open his briefcase and pulled out the paperwork he needed to study before a morning conference call. Deliberately pulling his mind away from Michigan and the future, he settled back on the couch and began to read.

\*\*\*\*

"Remember, if you run ahead, that's it. We'll go right back home."

"I know, Mom, I know." Brittani, dressed in a pink princess costume, rolled her eyes. She clutched the plastic tote bag tightly, eager to join the other children trick-or-treating in her parents' neighborhood. This tradition was firmly fixed. Miranda and Brittani walked until the bag was full or they tired of going door-to-door. Back at the house, her father would be building a fire in the family room fireplace and her mother would be putting the finishing touches on her made-from-scratch hot cocoa.

One thing had changed. Miranda hung back on the main sidewalk as Brittani ran up on the porches by herself. Standing with the other parents, she realized it wouldn't be long until her little girl was too big to do this anymore. The fun of spending the evening at her grandparents' would fade as Brittani discovered boys and Halloween parties.

And she'd be alone, left to worry until the door opened and Brittani came home.

*I miss you, Rik.*

The memory of his touch, his voice, his concern was so vivid she wouldn't have been surprised to turn around and see him behind her with that crooked smile on his face. She'd lean back against him, accept the comfort of his embrace as her worries became shared concerns.

"Look, Mom!" Brittani bounced up to her, the bag of candy bouncing against her leg. "I got a hamburger coupon!"

"We'll use it tomorrow," Miranda promised. "Are you done now or do you want to go to a few more houses?"

"I'm cold." Brittani handed her mother the colorful coupon and clutched her bag with both hands. "I hope Grandma makes some popcorn, too."

The two piles of candy on the living room grew steadily larger as Brittani divided her haul. The big candy bars would be distributed by Miranda as she saw fit. The miniatures went into several snack-size plastic bags that Brittani could grab from as she wanted.

"Tara's dad eats all her chocolate bars," Brittani confided as she reached the end of the bag.

"Oh, he does?" Miranda had been hearing a lot about the fathers of her daughter's friends. She dreaded the moment when Brittani would push to know why she didn't have a father in her life–almost as much as she dreaded the making the revelation when Rik came for Thanksgiving.

"Yeah." Brittani peeled the wrapper from a piece of taffy. "And he bought a new car. A fancy one that talks to him."

Miranda hid a smile. In Brittani's world, the car was actually speaking. She wasn't about to explain audible GPS and the other fancy tricks upscale autos offered.

The rest of the evening passed quickly. Brittani's yawns were deeper and closer together by the time they said goodbye and headed for their own place.

Miranda's usual routine didn't stop her thoughts from returning to Rik and whatever the future might hold. The bath that usually helped her sleep didn't work, and she ended up on the sofa, watching old reruns of sitcoms. Finally, she did the math in her head and realized that he was probably still awake thanks to the difference in time zones.

His phone rang and rang. After the fifth ring, she heard his voice.

"I'm sorry to miss your call," the recording informed her. "Leave your name and number and I'll in touch as soon as possible."

She shouldn't have called, she decided as she finally slid between the sheets a few minutes later. Just because she missed him didn't mean he felt the same way. And the sooner she realized that, the better.

Chapter Seventeen

Rik stared at the computer screen, re-reading Miranda's short e-mail, trying to figure out exactly what she wanted him to do.

"Brittani and I are doing fine and looking forward to Thanksgiving. Hope everything is going well for you, too."

It was the middle of November, and this was the first communication they'd had. His hopes were raised when he saw her phone number among his missed calls, but when he'd called back, she'd ignored it. He regularly checked her out on Internet, and knew she'd received a promotion to a supervisory position. He also saw her name listed as a PTA officer at Brittani's school. He'd learned that from her local newspaper's website; along with the article was a picture. Miranda's hair was shorter and the smile on her face looked real.

Doubt coursed through him. Was the formality of the e-mail a subtle signal that she'd found someone else?

Without giving himself time to second-guess himself, he went on-line and found a florist in her hometown. Using a form on the website, he ordered two dozen roses, half yellow and half red, to be delivered the next day. Surely that would break the silence.

****

"Okay, tell all."

Sandy, the secretary for Miranda's office, met her at the door as Miranda returned from lunch.

"What are you talking about?"

"A delivery guy showed up while you were gone. Go check your desk."

Frowning, Miranda walked down the short hallway to her office. She stopped in the doorway, surprised by the crystal vase filled with velvet-petaled roses. With slow steps, she walked over, pulled the little envelope from the plastic holder tucked into the vase and eased the card out. She blinked dampness from her eyes as she read the words.

"I still love you and the offer stands. Rik."

*The offer stands.*

His phrasing was discreet enough for the card to be seen in a work setting, but like Rik, also direct and to the point. The offer was marriage and the family life she so wanted for their daughter.

She took a deep breath, wishing she had a good friend to discuss the situation with. Her friendships were casual, revolving around work or Brittani's activities. At one time she could have confided in her mother, but Mary Coulsen was the last person she wanted to talk to now. Her mother wouldn't hesitate to tell her dad, which would open the can of worms she'd slammed the lid on.

"So?" Sandy hovered behind her. "You going to tell me who your secret admirer is?"

"Nope." Miranda tucked the card in her jacket pocket. "The cool thing about having a secret admirer is that no one gets to know. Now could you pull the file on that cemetery in the Upper Peninsula that may hold Native American remains?"

**** 

The roses were long faded by the time Miranda ran shivering from the Detroit airport parking garage to the terminal. Rik's plane would be landing in a few minutes and she wanted to be there to greet him. If she felt the same jolt in her system when she saw him again, experienced the same longing to hold and be held by him, the talk they'd have on the ride home would be different than the one she'd been planning since her return to Michigan.

She watched as other holiday travelers deplaned, waiting to catch a glimpse of the man she'd been thinking about nearly constantly for the past 48 hours. Finally the last small group came down the jet way and there he was. Miranda realized by looks sent his way that she wasn't the only woman to appreciate the way he looked in his black suit and cream tie, so different than the tees and jeans she was accustomed to seeing him wear.

A thrill of pride ran through her; Rik was here for her. He walked quickly over, wrapped his arms around her without hesitation and kissed her in a totally inappropriate way for an airport gate area.

"I've been waiting to do this ever since I got on that damn thing," Rik whispered when the kiss finally ended. Miranda nodded, too full of surprise, happiness and unmistakable wanting to speak.

Her heart soared as he took her hand and led the way to the baggage area. She loved him, in a deeper, better way that she had ten years ago. She loved the responsible, caring man he'd grown into. Snuggled against him, she didn't feel the cold as they crossed the wide lanes that separated the parking garage from the terminal. He refused her offer to let him drive when she held up the keys toward him.

"I'd feel much better if you drove," he said. "This is your city and you know your way around."

Miranda hid her surprise as she slid into the driver's seat. Maybe his insistence on being behind the wheel in Colorado last summer really was from his concern over the government car, and not a need to be in control.

"I've made reservations at a hotel closer to your parents' home," Rik said, "and tomorrow I'll have a rental car. Things will be easier if I have my own wheels."

"I was a little surprised you came on a commercial flight. I thought you might fly into the small airport we used last summer.'

Rik laughed. "I prefer to let others worry about storms and ice on the wings. This is a vacation, and I intend to treat it as one."

The radio provided a soft background as they covered the miles. Miranda kept her eyes on the highway even though she sensed Rik studying her. She wondered what he thought of her new look. To celebrate her promotion, she and her mother had treated themselves to a makeover day. By the end of the six hours, her hair had been cut into a short bob with highlights. She'd enjoyed her first hot rock massage and a cheerful cosmetologist had introduced her to a new makeup palette.

She had taken care with her clothes today. In deference to the weather, she'd worn a black wool skirt, red sweater and her favorite black calf boots. Gold hoop earrings glittered from the edge of her bob, and a locket with photos of Brittani hung around her neck. She'd even misted on a new perfume she'd discovered.

Not that she'd fixed herself up for him. Her parents were expecting them for a late dinner, and Brittani would seize any opportunity to dress up and make her mother follow suit.

The upscale hotel Rik had chosen had plush carpeting, elegant furniture and the sort of quiet that fine establishments specialized in. Although she'd planned to stay in the lobby and wait until Rik took his suitcase to his room, she accepted his invitation to accompany him after she realized he was booked into the executive suite.

"This place is gorgeous," she breathed as she took in the sumptuous surroundings.

"All I ask is a comfortable bed and plenty of hot water," Rik replied as he unpacked. "I might care about something more tomorrow. I've put in some long nights on top of long days to pull off a few days of freedom."

And there it was, one more difference. Miranda realized Rik took places like this for granted, while she was more accustomed to inexpensive motels that let children stay free.

Driving to her parents' house fifteen minutes later, she wondered how her childhood home looked to him. She loved its cozy bedrooms and familiar living room where her family had played board games on wintry, no-school days. The ranch house that Rik's family occupied was a virtual mansion compared to the vinyl-sided Cape Cod where she'd been raised.

Her father was at the door, looking through one of its glass panes as if in waiting. His greeting to Rik was both cordial and reserved. Miranda understood; she wasn't sure what this weekend would bring either.

"Good evening, Mrs. Coulsen." Rik bent his head in greeting and offered the ribbon-wrapped package he'd brought from the hotel.

Her mother smiled. "A gift? How thoughtful."

Miranda held back as the niceties were observed. Brittani would be home any moment from the ice skating trip with her Scout troop. This was the perfect time for her parents to get to know Rik a bit and size him up. And she intended to let that happen.

****

"So there I was, up in that tree stand with a big buck scratching his back not four feet beneath me. The tree was shaking so hard I was afraid to shoot, and that was that."

Her father ended his story with a bout of laughter; Miranda was pleased to hear Rik join in. She'd occupied herself in the kitchen for the last half-hour getting a head start on preparations for the next day. She'd managed to convince her mother to join the men by the fireplace. She wanted time to think almost as much as she wanted her parents to carry on a normal conversation with the man she loved.

She loved him, and not only for giving her the incredible gift of their daughter. She loved to be kissed by him. She loved the rumble of his voice and the feel of his fingers stroking her hair.

She longed to tell him so.

"Mom?" Brittani popped in through the back door. "Can I spend the night with Tara?"

"Not tonight, honey. Tomorrow's a big day."

Wiping her hands on the towel hanging from the refrigerator handle, Miranda headed out the door to talk to Tara's mother. Together they promised the two disappointed children that they could have a sleep-over the following weekend, complete with delivered pizza and their choice of movie.

"Bye, Tara!" Brittani shouted her farewell as she ran through the frosty air back into the house. Miranda hurried behind her; she wanted to be the one to tell her they had a visitor.

She was too late. By the time she made it inside and shut the door, Brittani had run into the family room to see her grandparents. Miranda joined them, not surprised that her daughter was peppering Rik with questions about when he'd gotten there and how long he was going to stay.

The huge yawn that stopped her in mid-sentence was Miranda's excuse to tuck her child into bed. It was time to formulate a plan on how to deliver news to Brittani that might make excited or make her hate them all.

Moments later, she rejoined the others.

"Get her all tucked in?"

Miranda nodded in response to her father's question.

"Did you cover her up well? It's supposed to get cold tonight," her mother added.

"And the furnace will keep us toasty warm." Miranda smiled and took the rocker by the fire. Her mom was like a mother hen, driven by her natural nurturing instincts.

The group sat watching the flames, the snaps and crackles of the wood the only sounds to break the silence. Finally Rik spoke.

"I'd like Brittani to learn this weekend that I'm her father. I hope that won't be a problem."

"We've discussed it." Her father's firm voice echoed in the room. "Both Mary and I believe it's time. I hope you'll be able to stay through the weekend because we've made an appointment with our family lawyer–for all of us."

Miranda watched Rik, waiting for his face to tighten or his hands to twitch the way they did when he was irritated. She was relieved that he seemed unconcerned about her father's high-handedness. She listened to the two men discuss what the weekend would bring, feeling oddly detached. It was as if they were talking about someone else's life, or maybe the contrived plot of a soap opera.

Yeah, her life would never be the same after tomorrow. But she was looking forward to the lightening of her spirit that their revelation would bring. Brittani deserved two parents; she'd cheated her of that long enough.

"Miranda?" Her mother's voice interrupted her musing and she could tell by Mom's tone that it wasn't the first time she'd spoken to her.

"I'm sorry. The fire had me practically hypnotized."

"Dad asked whether you'd like him to take Rik back to his hotel. It's been snowing for quite a while."

Oh, no, that wasn't about to happen.

"I'll stick to the main streets," she said as she rose and headed for the closet that held their coats. "It's only supposed to give us an inch or two anyway."

Rik was beside her, helping her with her coat, before the last words left her lips. As soon as the door shut behind them, his arm wrapped around her waist. Miranda leaned into him, all too aware of the tight body pressed against her.

His presence filled the space between as she drove toward the hotel. Her senses were heightened; the scent that was so Rik was driving her crazy. She kept both hands on the wheel and her eyes on the road even after he laid a hand on her thigh, her mind whirling.

"I'd ask you in, but I don't want you to be out on the streets if the weather gets worse," he said as she pulled into the hotel parking lot.

Miranda was both disappointed and relieved. That kiss at the airport had tipped the scales in Rik's favor. If he'd asked, she'd have gone upstairs with him after calling her parents to say she didn't feel confident on the icy streets. But going straight home gave her a chance to talk to them without any chance of Brittani's overhearing.

"Remember what I said about the right time and place?" Rik asked, his hand massaging the nape of her neck.

Miranda nodded.

"I still mean it." He tipped her face toward him and dropped a light kiss on her lips. "You can count on that."

One more light kiss and he was slipping out of the car, walking across the lot to the lobby doors. Miranda watched him go, snowflakes dancing around him. Sighing, she shifted the transmission into drive and headed back to her parents' house and the bedroom where she'd sleep alone.

\*\*\*\*

"Is he your boyfriend now?

Miranda stopped rinsing the cut potatoes at Brittani's innocent query. That was a question she hadn't expected but probably should have been prepared. All too aware of her responsibility as a mom, she hadn't let any of the few men she'd dated meet her daughter. This was exactly the reason why.

"Mr. Hallowell and I are good friends," she said. "His family isn't getting together for Thanksgiving so I thought he might enjoy being with us."

"Oh." Brittani jumped off the kitchen stool and grabbed a carrot from the vegetable plate her grandmother was assembling. "It would be cool if he was."

Mary waited until her granddaughter had skipped out of the room to say, "I heard for a week last summer about Rik's cowboy boots and his private plane. You don't have to worry about her not taking to him, that's for sure."

Miranda set the colander of potatoes on the counter and turned to her mother with a deep exhalation of breath.

"Mom, sometimes I'm sure we're doing the right thing and other times, I think there might be a better way for her to learn the truth. What if she hates me for keeping her from Rik? She's too young to understand why I did what I did."

"Don't underestimate your daughter," Mary replied. "I suspect she has an inkling. You've never had a man to our house before and Rik's been here twice now. Trust yourself and trust her."

Her mother's words stayed with her throughout the big dinner and the afternoon that followed. Her father and Rik sat side by side on the couch watching the football game while Brittani played a video game at their feet on her handheld game device. The scene might have come from a sugary television ad, one that extolled the virtues of digital cameras or certain soft drinks.

Supper was a light meal of turkey sandwiches and chips. After the table had been cleared, Bill said, "I hate to leave good company but I promised Al I'd let his dog out while he's out of town. Mary, you coming with me?"

Miranda almost wanted to jump in the car and join them. The time had finally come for their heart-to-heart with Brittani. She wondered if Rik was as nervous as she was.

If so, it didn't show up in his voice as he asked Brittani to sit beside him. Miranda took her favorite place in the rocker and smiled at her daughter.

"Sometimes," she said, "grown-ups make mistakes. We think we're doing the right thing and then we find out we're not.

"I know you wonder why you don't have a father in your life like your friends do. The truth is, that was one of those times when I thought what I decided was right but now I know it wasn't." She took a deep breath and continued before she chickened out. "Your father is sitting right next to you, honey. He didn't know he had a little girl until I saw him again last summer, and he really wants to be your daddy now."

Brittani turned and smiled at Rik.

"I already knew it!" Her tone was smug.

"What do you mean, you already knew?" Miranda asked.

"Because I heard Gramma and Grandpops talking last night when you two went away."

"You did?" A sinking feeling grew in Miranda. Exactly what had her daughter overheard?

"Uh huh. When I got thirsty. I came down to ask Gramma for a drink and heard Grandpops talking about what would happen at Christmas." She turned back to Rik. "Are you really going to take me to your ranch?"

Stricken, Miranda stared at Rik. They hadn't talked about custody, holidays or visitation. Not yet anyway. She wondered if he'd broken their agreement and gotten his lawyer involved. Her heart clenched. No way could she celebrate Christmas without her daughter, whether it was thousands of miles away or just down the street.

"I'd love to have you visit and meet everyone in Armont," Rik said, "but your mother and I have to do a lot of planning first. Maybe I could come back here for Christmas."

"Maybe." Miranda stepped in before Brittani could start asking questions. "Right now, I want to tell you a story about what happened when I went to visit a friend on a train."

"Were you old like now?"

"I was pretty young," Miranda answered, tamping down a laugh. "I'd just finished high school and I was going all the way to California all by myself. I went to Denver on one train, spent the night and then got onto another train." She glanced at Rik. "There was a really cute boy."

"My dad!" Delight colored Brittani's voice.

"Your father." Miranda nodded.

"I thought your mom was the prettiest girl I'd ever seen," Rik cut in. "She needed help with her suitcases, and I figured if I did, she'd give me a kiss to say thank you."

Brittani's eyes widened. "Did you, Mom?"

"Not then. Not until we spent so much time together that I knew this was the one person I'd love forever and forever. But your daddy had to go back to Colorado and I had to go to college, and it took all this time for us to find each other again."

She watched Brittani's face become sober, and wondered what her daughter was about to ask. "So are you gonna get married now?"

One thing about her daughter, she didn't beat around the bush, Miranda realized as she fished around for the right thing to say. Of all the questions she'd expected, this wasn't even on the list.

"Someday." Rik's voice was firm. "That's what I hope anyway. Your mom and I have a lot to talk about before we decide something as important as that."

"Oh." A pause and then a hopeful, "Can I get a pony if you do?"

Miranda's amusement was underscored by Rik's rich laughter. The moment she'd dreaded was over and the world hadn't ended.

In typical kid fashion, Brittani accepted her mother's "We'll see" and asked if she could call Tara and tell her the news. Permission granted, she grabbed the cordless phone and headed to her bedroom.

"I think we have our daughter's blessing," Rik said, patting the couch beside him. "I've already had a talk with your dad."

Miranda stayed put in the rocker. This discussion called for a clear head, not the rush of hormones from being close to him. Dad hadn't said a word about any talk about Rik's intentions, although he'd definitely been friendlier than on Rik's first trip here.

"We both agreed that youthful mistakes can be forgiven," he continued. "He even confessed to a few that he's put behind him."

"Such as?"

Rik grinned. "I promised I wouldn't tell. But you might want to ask him about a drag race out on Rt. 241."

"My father in a drag race?"

"You didn't hear it from me. The point is that at the end of the conversation, we both agreed that winter weddings are nice."

In a quick move, Rik was off the couch and kneeling by the rocker.

"Miranda Coulsen, would you marry me?"

He fumbled in his pocket and pulled out a small hinged box. Miranda gasped when he opened it to expose a brilliant diamond and ruby ring.

"Rik, I...this is so sudden," Miranda stammered.

"I've thought about nothing but you since you left Colorado. I may be a little thick-skulled sometimes but I finally realized I'd been using work as a substitute for life. The thrill of the deal isn't there anymore. If I never attend another gala or art opening, I'll be fine.

"I want to wake up with you beside me and our child down the hall. I want to give her that pony she wants, and sisters and brothers too if you want that. Please, Miranda, marry me."

The break in his voice with those final words loosened the wall she'd put around her heart. The pain she'd carried was driven away by her love for him, her deep wanting for the life they could have together.

She'd spent the last 10 years being ultra-careful, living the same kind of half life as him. Now the future opened to her as a dazzling panorama, full of promise.

She nodded, too unsure of her voice to speak. As he slid the ring on her finger, it seemed so right; the last of her doubt faded.

"Spring," she managed after Rik's answering kiss. "I only intend to do this once, so I want to do it right."

"You're killing me," Rik muttered as he lifted her from the rocker and over to the couch. He slid her onto his lap and wrapped his arms around her. "I don't think I can wait another six months."

"My folks will be back soon," she whispered, her fingers sliding beneath her shirt. "I don't think they'd mind if I took a little longer at the hotel this time."

Rik's answer was that laugh she loved and a kiss full of promise that took her breath away.

## Chapter Eighteen

The Colorado sky was a spectacular blue, the ranch lawn filled with everything necessary for a perfect wedding from rows of chairs to the caterer's tent. Miranda stood inside the house in her lacy ivory gown, butterflies dancing in her stomach. Her father stepped up to her, smiled and said, "It's not too late to back out, you know."

Miranda laughed. "Rik's already bought Brittani that pony, so I don't think she'd take it well if I became a runaway bride."

"Then I guess we'd better get this show on the road."

Miranda slipped her hand onto her father's bent arm, took a deep breath and stepped out the front door. The string quartet began playing the traditional wedding march and Brittani led the procession in her flower girl dress.

Blinking back tears at the sight of Rik in a black tuxedo, Miranda walked down the white runner to meet her groom under an arch of flowers created for the occasion. His brother stood beside him as best man and a beaming Rosie waited as Miranda's matron of honor.

The ceremony passed in a blur. Miranda remembered the minister's short talk on love and family, and Brittani's cheer as Rik said "I do" at the appropriate time. His mother beaming as they headed back down that aisle as husband and wife was outshone only by her own mother's teary smile.

"How long do we have to stay?" Rik whispered to her as they took their seats at the table of honor.

"Long enough to have a toast and cut the cake," Miranda whispered back.

"Brittani's been pretty insistent that she wants a little sister. I'd like to get started on that right away."

Miranda shook her head and turned her attention to Ron, who was offering a toast for their health and happiness. That was followed by a toast from her father and then Rik's mother. Finally they cut the first piece of wedding cake and brought gales of giggles from Brittani when they made a mess of feeding it to each other.

They made their escape shortly after, driving to Denver for their wedding night and then heading off for a Hawaiian honeymoon while Rik's mother got acquainted with her granddaughter.

It wasn't until much later that evening that Miranda, snuggled against Rik's naked body in the wide bed of the honeymoon suite, said, "Did you see who caught my bouquet?"

"Please tell me it wasn't my mother. I'm not sure I'm ready for a stepfather."

Miranda playfully slapped his chest.

"No, silly. Take another guess."

"Hazel? She'll be quite a catch the way she cooks."

"I guess I'll have to tell you then."

"And it was?" Rik asked, his hands moving in lazy circles across her back.

"Your good friend Junie. And the first person she showed it to was Bret."

Rik chuckled. "Good for her. He's played fast and loose long enough. Remind me to tell Rosie to stock up on champagne and get that cabin ready."

Miranda sighed and curled into his body. She was finally where she belonged, with the man fate had chosen for her. As she slid into sleep, she decided it was time to share her final secret.

That little brother or sister their daughter wanted was already on the way.

## About The Author

Cat Shaffer, the daughter of a poet and a teacher/librarian, grew up in northwest Ohio, finally saw the light and moved to Kentucky, the land of beautiful horses and far better weather. She lives with a dignified but ultra-sneaky cat and rambunctious dog, and could not continue to live if coffee disappeared from the planet. Check out her website at www.catshaffer.com.

Did you enjoy this book?

Share your opinion by telling your friends or writing a review!

**Other books by Cat Shaffer:**

*Keeping Secrets*, contemporary romance

*Bittersweet,* historical romantic suspense

*Kentucky Blues,* contemporary romantic suspense

*No Safe Place*, contemporary romantic suspense

*Her Hired Man,* humorous contemporary romance

*Dixie White and the Seven Dates,* humorous contemporary romance

*Academy for Losers,* young adult paranormal